JOURNEY TO PARADISE

Lauren is on holiday in the Bahamas when a tropical storm breaks out. She is left in the care of Glenn, a very attractive American who takes shelter with her. They fall in love — but the problem is, he is the boyfriend of her best friend Anna. Lauren returns home racked with guilt, vowing to forget Glenn, but he has other ideas. Can they find a way of being together without hurting Anna?

DAWN BRIDGE

JOURNEY TO PARADISE

Complete and Unabridged

LINFORD
Leicester

First published in Great Britain in 2009

First Linford Edition
published 2012

British Library CIP Data

Bridge, Dawn.
Journey to paradise. - -
(Linford romance library)
1. Love stories.
2. Large type books.
I. Title II. Series
823.9′2–dc23

ISBN 978–1–4448–1179–7

Published by
F. A. Thorpe (Publishing)
Anstey, Leicestershire

Set by Words & Graphics Ltd.
Anstey, Leicestershire
Printed and bound in Great Britain by
T. J. International Ltd., Padstow, Cornwall

This book is printed on acid-free paper

A Chance Encounter

This is going to be an experience of a lifetime, Lauren thought, as she arrived at the airport and stepped out of the car. She glanced around the dark parking bays and then into the daylight beyond, trying to take everything in, wanting this feeling of excitement to be imprinted on her memory. Today she was flying to the other side of the world!

'I'll wait till you've checked in. Then I'd better go,' Michael said. 'Sorry I can't stay any longer, Lauren.'

'That's all right. I know you have to work. I'm just glad I've got such a kind and helpful brother.'

'That's what big brothers are for,' Michael said, as he humped Lauren's heavy suitcase on to a trolley. 'I promised Mum I'd take care of you.'

'I know and you always have. She'd

have been so proud of you.' Lauren couldn't help wiping a tear from her eye.

'Don't start upsetting yourself now.'

Michael gave her a hug.

'Just have a good holiday and enjoy yourself. That's what Mum would have wanted.'

'You're right. And driving me to the airport has really helped. I hate having to drag all my luggage on the train and a taxi would have cost a fortune. And I do need to save some money. The fare to Nassau was so expensive.'

'You'll have to ask your boss to give you a rise.'

'I don't think he'll do that.'

'Why not? You work hard enough and you don't get paid for all the overtime you do.'

'I know. But he'd say, 'I don't expect you to go on expensive holidays.' And after all, I don't *have* to visit my friend in the Bahamas.'

'I suppose so. But Sis, you couldn't miss out on the holiday of a lifetime!'

'That's what I thought,' Lauren said excitedly, as they arrived at the front of the check-in queue. She checked her suitcase in, and was pleased to hear that her flight was due to take off on time. 'You'd better go,' she urged Michael. 'I don't want you arriving late for work.'

'Are you sure you'll be OK?' Michael said.

'Of course. And thanks so much for the lift,' Lauren said, kissing her brother on the cheek.

'Have a lovely holiday. Give Anna my love and don't get up to any mischief!'

'As if I would,' Lauren laughed. 'I'm a big girl now, nearly twenty-five. I can take care of myself.'

'I hope so, but you haven't flown on your own before, and it is quite a long flight.'

'It'll soon pass, and Anna will be at the airport to meet me, so stop worrying.'

'All right. Bye Lauren.' He gave his sister another hug and walked away. She waved until he was out of sight.

* * *

What do I do now, Lauren wondered. She'd been so excited about this day, had been planning it for ages, but suddenly she didn't feel quite so brave, now Michael had left. She'd never been on a long haul flight before. And she'd never travelled alone. She'd flown to Europe and had crossed the Channel by boat, and been on Eurostar, but always with somebody. This was her first trip on her own. Still, when she got there, she wouldn't be on her own, she'd be staying with Anna. She was really looking forward to seeing her friend again.

But she had to get this journey over first. She hoped it would soon pass and then she'd be four thousand miles away on an island where it always seemed to be summer. Anna made it sound like Paradise; sunshine, palm trees, turquoise sea and white, sandy beaches.

After her friend had moved to Nassau a year ago to take up a teaching post in a private school, she'd kept in frequent contact with Lauren and, when she'd invited her for a holiday, Lauren couldn't resist.

She glanced at her watch. It was time to go through Passport Control, if she wanted to have the chance of looking round the Duty Free Shop.

Ten minutes later she was in the perfume section, browsing amongst the shelves, studying the different bottles, trying to decide which to test. She stepped backwards, and felt her heel come into contact with something.

'Ouch!'

Lauren spun round and looked up into a pair of deep blue eyes. 'That hurt,' the man said, rubbing his foot.

'I'm so sorry,' she stammered. 'I didn't see you there.'

'I guess you didn't. I wouldn't like to think that you did that on purpose.' He smiled then and Lauren blushed. She couldn't help noticing his rich American accent, his broad shoulders, immaculate navy suit, and dark brown hair. He had an air of self-confidence and affluence about him. She suddenly felt very aware of her own inexpensive jumper and trousers, and dark, unruly curls which seemed to have a mind of their own, however much she tried to tame them. 'I was trying to decide which perfume to buy,' she said lamely.

Surely you can come up with something better than that, she told herself. You've just bumped into the most gorgeous man you've ever seen and that's all you can think of to say?

'I was doing the same,' he answered.

'Oh.' Lauren tried not to sound deflated. He must be buying it for his wife or girlfriend. Well, would you really expect someone who looks like that, to be unattached?

'I think I've made my choice,' he said, holding out an ornately-shaped bottle. 'Do you like this one?'

'Yes it's one of my favourites.'

'Good. I expect it will be okay then. And it was nice meeting you, even if it did cause me some pain! Enjoy your flight.'

'Thank you. I hope your foot will be better.'

Lauren watched as the man went to the checkout. He must be travelling on his own, she thought. Maybe he's going away on business and is buying the perfume for his partner. Oh well, lucky old partner.

* * *

One hour later Lauren had boarded the plane. She was sitting by a window with an empty seat beside her. She took out a travel magazine from the pocket of the seat in front of her and proceeded to study it, trying to take her mind off the impending flight. Just then, an elderly lady heaved herself into the spare seat.

'Thank goodness,' she sighed. 'I've made it.'

'Were you late, then?' Lauren asked.

'Yes, we got stuck in a traffic jam.

Had a mad dash to get here in time. You know what they're like on the check-ins. Won't let you past if you're a minute late.'

They made polite conversation for a while as the cabin staff prepared for take-off.

The pilot revved the engine and Sadie, Lauren's fellow passenger, said, 'I'm terrified of flying, but my granddaughter emigrated to Nassau five years ago, so I feel I have to go and see her and my new great grandchild while I'm still fit enough.'

'That's nice for you,' Lauren replied. 'I mean, going to see your family. I'm a bit nervous of flying too,' she confided.

'It'll be all right once we're up. Ooh . . . we're going now.' Sadie screwed her face up and leant back in her seat.

Lauren held on to the arm rest and closed her eyes. Then suddenly, the plane was levelling out and flying into the sunshine above the clouds.

'That wasn't too bad, was it, dear?'

Sadie remarked, leaning over Lauren to peer out of the window.

'No. Quite smooth really.'

'I think I'll read my book now. You don't mind, do you? It's a love story. Nothing like a bit of romance to take your mind off things.'

Lauren was glad. The old lady was pleasant enough, but she didn't really want to spend the whole flight making polite conversation.

She took her own book out of her bag and settled down for a long read, but found it hard to concentrate. Her mind was full of thoughts about the holiday ahead of her.

* * *

Lauren had known Anna since they were children. She was three years younger and had looked up to Anna as a big sister. When Lauren was six, her father was killed in a motor cycle accident. Her mother was devastated and couldn't bear to stay in the same area where she had been so happy with Lauren's father. She took her two children, Lauren and her brother, Michael, to another town and they moved into the flat next door to where Anna, an only child, lived with her parents. The two girls and Lauren's brother, Michael, who was the same age as Anna, became the best of friends. This continued throughout their school and college years, and afterwards, when they started work. Lauren worked in an office and Anna had become a teacher.

Then, Lauren and Michael's mother died suddenly at the age of fifty and it was Anna who comforted the orphaned brother and sister.

Lauren had always nursed a secret hope that one day a romance would develop between Anna and Michael, but, to her surprise, Anna got involved with a friend of a teacher at the school where she worked. Soon they were engaged, and Lauren was looking forward to being her best friend's bridesmaid. Then came the shock.

Anna discovered that her fiancé, Rob, had been unfaithful to her. She was devastated and couldn't forgive him, even though he said he was sorry and promised that it would never happen again.

Anna just wanted to get right away and discovered that they were recruiting English teachers to work in the Bahamas. She applied and was fortunate enough to obtain a teaching position in Nassau. Lauren had supported Anna in making her decision, although she knew that she would miss her friend a great deal.

'You'll have to come and visit me,' Anna had said.

Lauren had agreed at the time, but thought it unlikely, as it would be too expensive. However, after Anna had settled down in Nassau, she again invited her friend.

Lauren discussed this with Michael and he agreed that it would be a good thing for her to go. 'After all, you haven't had a proper holiday for years, not since before Mum died, when we all went to Majorca. You deserve a break.'

'I wish you could come too.'

'That's out of the question. I couldn't get the time off work when Anna wants you to go. The summer's a very busy period. Besides, I don't want to impose on Anna. And anyway, I'm trying to save my money.'

Lauren wondered what her big brother was saving up for, but she didn't like to ask.

She thought back over the events of the past years. Life had been hard when they were children. After her father's death, money had been tight. Their mother had worked long hours night and day as a nurse, so that Michael could go to university. No-one had been aware that she had a heart problem, but Lauren had often wondered if her mother knew about her condition. She'd tried to pack so much into the last few months of her life. The three of them had gone to

Majorca and had a marvellous holiday. 'We'll have the time of our lives,' she'd said, 'before you two settle down and get married.'

Lauren had answered quickly, 'I'm not planning to do that.'

Her mother had replied, 'You can't spend all your life pining for what might have been, Lauren. You've got to move forward.'

'I know that,' she'd retorted sharply.

Michael had kept quiet and Lauren wondered if he'd had a broken romance, too, maybe when he had been away at University. She'd never been able to understand why someone as good-looking and kind-hearted as him was still unattached. When she'd said this to him, he'd just shrugged it off and laughed.

Soon after they returned from Majorca their mother had died. Were there any warning signs they had missed? Lauren asked herself this over and over again and she would never know the answer.

* * *

It was now Anna's summer holiday from school and she was delighted that Lauren had agreed to come for a holiday. In her last email she had said mysteriously, 'There's someone I'd like you to meet.'

Had Anna found herself a new man? Lauren wondered. She deserved to be happy after the way she'd been treated by Rob.

'That was a big sigh.' The elderly woman interrupted Lauren's thoughts. 'You're not getting bored already, are you? We've a long way to go yet.'

'Oh, sorry. I was just thinking.'

'Couldn't have been very happy thoughts. Oh, I shouldn't have said that. I don't want to intrude.'

'You're not,' Lauren said politely.

'Boyfriend problems, dear? Oh, there I go again,' Sadie stopped and put her hand to her mouth. 'Nosy . . . that's my trouble. Just tell me to mind my own business.'

'No. That's all right. Actually, I was thinking about my friend. The one I'm going to see in Nassau. It's Anna who has the problems.'

'Do you want to talk about them?'

For the next few minutes Lauren told Sadie about Anna's broken engagement. Then the elderly lady asked, 'Have you got a boyfriend, dear?'

'No. Not at the moment.' I wouldn't mind having one, who looked like that man whose foot I stood on, though, she thought. Then she chided herself, whatever made you think of him?

'I am surprised. A good-looking girl like you, with your curls and those pretty green eyes,' Sadie was saying. 'I'd have thought all the young men would be queuing up.'

Lauren blushed and laughed. 'I wish they were.'

'I'm sure you'll find a nice young man soon, dear. Maybe you'll meet somebody in Nassau.'

Lauren smiled and looked down at her book as if she wanted to continue reading. Sadie took the hint and turned back to hers.

* * *

Did she really want to meet someone, Lauren asked herself, after her disastrous relationship all those years ago, when she had been little more than a teenager? She'd thought Jake was special, but he wasn't. She'd tried to block the whole episode from her mind, but that had made it difficult for her to relax in any other man's company.

She wondered if it was because of her that Michael was still unattached. After their mother's death, he'd returned home to their old flat to keep Lauren company.

'You don't want to live here all on your own,' he'd said. 'Besides, you need looking after.'

'I'm grown-up,' she pointed out. 'And we could sell the flat.'

'What do we want to sell the flat for? It'll be cheaper for us to stay together, at least for the time being.'

That had been more than two years ago. It had taken Lauren that amount of time to come to terms with her mother's death.

Even now, she could easily get upset about it.

'I don't think you ever really get over something like that,' Michael had said.

He was right, but you had to carry on with your life and that was what she was doing now. She was determined she was going to enjoy this holiday.

Anna's life hadn't been easy either, but she'd made a real effort and sounded happy when Lauren had last spoken to her on the phone. She couldn't wait to see her friend. They'd have so much to talk about.

* * *

Lauren and Michael had gone to see Anna off at the airport when she'd first gone to the Bahamas. Anna had looked small and sad as they'd waved her through Passport Control. After her broken engagement, it seemed as if she had shrunk, she'd lost so much weight. Lauren had been really worried about her.

'You should see a doctor,' she'd advised.

'When I get away from here, I'll be fine,' Anna had said.

To Lauren's relief, Anna had been right. She quickly settled into a new routine in Nassau. The children there were much easier to teach than those in England, and she loved the more relaxed way of life, she said. She kept on inviting her friend to come and visit her, until in the end Lauren gave in and arranged this holiday.

'If you like it in Nassau, you could look for a job, too,' Anna had said.

'I'm sure I will like it,' Lauren had told her, 'but I don't think I want to leave England. Besides, Michael would be all on his own.'

'He's old enough to look after himself, you know, Lauren. Anyway, I expect he'll find himself a girlfriend soon. I'm surprised he's stayed single this long.'

'You're probably right,' Lauren had agreed.

* * *

Lauren closed her eyes. The motion of the plane had made her sleepy. Soon she was dreaming of swimming in a turquoise sea, with the sun beating down on her. There was someone beside her, but she couldn't see his face.

Lauren was awakened by Sadie, who was thrusting a tray of food at her. She felt quite disappointed that her dream had ended.

'Sorry dear, I didn't realise you were asleep. You do want lunch, I suppose?'

'Oh, that's all right. And yes, I am rather hungry. It seems a long time since breakfast.' She put the food down on the tray in front of her and started to open up the dishes.

'By the way, I'm Sadie. I forgot to introduce myself,' she said.

'I'm Lauren.'

'What a lovely name. You don't hear it very often. Wasn't there a film star with that name? But you probably don't remember. It was long before your time.'

'Yes, Lauren Bacall. I was named after her. She was married to Humphrey Bogart, who was my granddad's favourite film star. When I was born, Granddad suggested the name to my mother and she liked it, so that's what I was christened.'

'That's interesting. Oh, I'm so glad I've got someone nice to talk to,' Sadie said. 'It makes the journey pass so much quicker.'

'I know what you mean,' Lauren agreed. She couldn't help thinking, though, that it would have been even better if the handsome American had been seated beside her.

Sadie and Lauren ate their lunch, chatting amicably. They discovered that they were both going to be in Nassau for two weeks and would be travelling home on the same flight. 'Let's hope we're sitting together then,' Sadie said. 'We'll be able to tell each other what we've been up to. And you never know, I might even see you around Nassau some time.'

When they had finished eating, Lauren decided to go and freshen up. She walked up the aisle, enjoying being able to stretch her legs. On her return, feeling that she needed further exercise, she went the long way round, but her foot caught in something and she lurched forward.

As she tried to regain her balance, there was some turbulence and her head hit the seat in front of her. 'Oh,' she gasped, stunned, clutching her forehead.

Dazed, she felt strong hands pulling her up. 'Are you okay?' a familiar masculine voice drawled. 'I'm so sorry, you must have caught your foot in my bag strap. Shall I call the stewardess?'

I must have concussion Lauren

thought, but that voice . . . it sounds like . . . No. It can't be . . . Why have I got that man on the brain? It must be the accent. He can't be the only American on this plane.

She tried to pull herself together. 'I'm all right,' she murmured weakly. She wanted to move away, but felt too dizzy.

'Look, sit down a minute,' the man said. 'You can have my seat.'

Lauren turned her head and gazed up into the deep blue eyes of the man whose foot she had trodden on in the Duty Free Shop.

Lauren Meets Her Friend

Lauren sank down in the seat feeling dazed. Was it because she'd bumped her head that she was feeling this way? Or was it due to the fact that this exceedingly attractive man was staring down at her with a look of concern on his face? But she wasn't too stunned to notice that the window seat next to his was empty, apart from his discarded jacket and laptop. She guessed that he, too, was on his own.

'I'm so sorry,' the man said again. 'Are you sure you're OK? I should have tucked my bag in properly. I got it out to look at some papers and must have forgotten to push it back.'

'I'm fine,' Lauren said. 'I just feel a bit disorientated. I'll be all right in a minute.' But, she thought, I won't be if you keep looking at me like that. She noticed his tanned face and hands, his brown hair, his deep blue eyes.

'I'll get the stewardess.' His voice was full of concern.

'No. I don't want to make a fuss.'

'But if you're hurt . . . '

'Please don't bother anyone,' Lauren said. 'I'm OK.' She stood up, trying to conceal how shaky she was feeling. 'You can sit down again. I'm going back to my own seat.'

'I'll come with you. Just to make sure nothing else happens.'

'I'll be fine.'

'Are you travelling alone? I mean . . . is there anybody to take care of you?'

'No. I'm not with anyone, but I am sitting next to a kindly lady, so don't worry about me.'

'But I shall. I don't make a habit of tripping girls up, even when they've stood on my foot,' he smiled.

Lauren's eyes met his. She could feel her heart thumping and it wasn't the knock on her head which was causing it.

'There's really no need,' she repeated.

‘Well, if you’re sure,’ he said, ‘I’ll let you go. But if you need anything, you only have to ask.’

‘Thank you.’

Lauren walked unsteadily back to her seat. When she got there she turned round and saw the man was still standing where she had left him.

* * *

Sadie stood up, moved aside and said, ‘What was that all about? Who is that man? Do you know him?’

Before Lauren could answer, Sadie patted her on the shoulder and apologised, ‘I’m sorry, there I go again, being nosy. It’s none of my business.’

‘I tripped over his bag and he helped me up, that’s all,’ Lauren told her.

Sadie scrutinised Lauren’s face. ‘So are you OK?’

‘Yes, thank you, but I am feeling tired. I think I’ll have a sleep for a while.’

‘A good idea. I’ll do the same when

I've freshened up.'

When, a few minutes later, Sadie hadn't returned, Lauren turned round and saw her talking to the American. He was looking in her direction, so she quickly turned back again. Whatever is she saying?

Sadie eventually came back, a look of glee on her face as she said, 'I've just told that nice young man that I'm keeping an eye on you. He sounded most concerned. Worried that he'd hurt you. He's American, you know, from New York. Has to travel on business backwards and forwards to the Bahamas as well as various other places.' Sadie paused, 'And . . . I couldn't help noticing that he isn't wearing a wedding ring. Still, I shouldn't keep prattling on. You want to sleep.'

Lauren smiled weakly and closed her eyes. Her head was throbbing now. She wasn't sure if it was the bump to her head which was causing it, or her feeling of embarrassment, or because of Sadie's endless chatter. Does this woman ever keep quiet, she wondered? Lauren was glad to have company on the flight, but she hadn't bargained on anybody trying to match-make her, even if it was with the only man she had fancied in quite a while. Anyway, Sadie was wrong, he did have somebody. He was buying her perfume.

But a little voice in her head said, 'You wouldn't mind if Sadie was right, though, would you?'

She silenced the voice by reminding herself that soon the flight would be over and she would never see him again. She didn't even know his name. It's amazing Sadie didn't find that out! On this thought, Lauren drifted back to sleep.

The rest of the flight passed uneventfully. The two women spent their time dozing, reading, and watching television, interspersed with another meal. Sadie made a point of going past the American again, and was disappointed that she couldn't get into conversation with him as he was sleeping, but

Lauren was glad. She didn't want to have any more embarrassing episodes.

* * *

Lauren's headache had gone and she was looking forward to meeting Anna in Nassau. She changed her watch to the local time, which was five hours behind London.

The landing was smooth. Sadie told Lauren not to wait for her when they got off the plane. 'I'm much too slow for you, dear. It's my legs, arthritis, you know. Look out for me on the return flight, though.'

Lauren promised she would. 'Have a lovely time with your family, Sadie. See you in two weeks.'

She hadn't expected to see the American again, but once, while waiting to reclaim her baggage, she spotted him across the other side of the turntable.

She noticed that he was looking at her, but she acted as if she were unaware of him.

Soon she found her baggage and set off to find Anna.

She had promised to meet her at the other side of the barrier, but as she walked through it she heard a loud-speaker announcing, 'Would Miss Lauren Drew please go to the Information Desk.'

She made her way there as quickly as she could, feeling worried, wondering what had happened.

The woman at the desk told her, 'Anna is very sorry she can't meet you, but she has sent a friend instead.'

'Hello,' said a tall, tanned woman, who was standing at the side of the counter, watching the arrivals. 'Are you Lauren? I'm Anna's friend, Catherine.'

'Pleased to meet you.' Lauren shook her hand. 'What's happened to Anna?'

'She's at the dentist. She's had a terrible toothache since yesterday. The only appointment she could get was for this afternoon. She's terribly sorry, but she was in agony, so I told her I would pick you up and take you to her flat. I hope you don't mind.'

'Of course not. And I hope Anna's OK. Toothache can be horrible.'

'Let me help you with your case.' Catherine picked it up and hauled it on to a trolley. 'My car's not far away.'

* * *

Soon they were travelling along the main road from the airport towards Anna's flat, past lush, exotic plants, casuarinas trees, oleander and bougainvillaea.

Lauren eagerly looked out, scarcely believing that at last she was in the Bahamas. The sun had never seemed so bright, or the sky so blue. Although the windows were open, the heat was overwhelming.

'Sorry I haven't got air conditioning,' Catherine remarked. 'Can't afford it on my salary.'

'Are you a teacher, too?' Lauren asked.

'Yes, at the same school as Anna.'

'How long have you lived here?'

‘This is my second year. I originally only intended staying just one, but I’ve met someone out here and we plan to get married in a few months.’

‘Oh, congratulations!’ Lauren exclaimed. ‘I hope you’ll be very happy.’

‘Thank you. I’m sure we will. I’m so lucky. Wonderful man, beautiful home, good job in a marvellous climate. What more could anyone want?’

Lauren didn’t know how to answer. Things like that didn’t seem to happen to her. Once her life had been so full of promise; then everything had changed. Her self-esteem had been shattered, and on top of that, there was the death of her mother. Lauren was only just emerging from a long, dark period and was now trying to rebuild her life. She guessed it was the same for Anna, after her broken engagement.

Soon they arrived at her friend’s apartment. Lauren looked at the white low-rise block, which was surrounded by colourful shrubs and bushes, so different from her home in England.

'Follow me,' Catherine said. 'We'll take the lift. It's too hot to walk up to the first floor with the luggage. I'll get you a cold drink. I think you must be needing one.'

'Yes. I am thirsty. It's this heat,' Lauren said. 'I'm not used to it.'

'I'll put the fan on for you. When Anna comes back, I expect she'll switch on the air conditioning. This is the hottest time of year, I'm afraid, but at least most places here are cool inside, not like London in a heatwave.'

They stepped out of the lift on to a spacious landing and Catherine ushered Lauren through a bright red door into Anna's flat.

'This is lovely,' she exclaimed, putting down her luggage and pausing to admire the multitude of pictures which were displayed on the walls of the entrance hall. 'It's like an art gallery. I recognise some of them as Anna's own work.'

'Yes, she likes to paint whenever she can. There's several more in the rest of the flat. The room you'll be sleeping in is where Anna does her painting. It's really big, plenty of space for a double bed and an easel and other art equipment. Come and see.'

Lauren wheeled her case through the hall, following Catherine into a light and airy bedroom.

'Leave your things in here. There's a small en-suite bathroom if you want to freshen up. I'll get some drinks. Will fruit juice be all right?'

'Fine. Thank you.'

Lauren gazed appreciatively around the room. Anna's done really well for herself, she reflected, finding this flat, and her friend Catherine seems very nice. I'm so pleased for her.

Half an hour later, as Lauren was admiring the view from the lounge window, she saw a blue car turn into the drive. 'That's Anna now,' Catherine said.

They went to the front door to greet her. Anna flung her arms around Lauren and hugged her. 'I'm so glad you're here. Sorry I couldn't meet you, but I know Catherine will have looked after you well.'

'She's been brilliant. So how was the dentist?'

'I feel a lot better now than I did a few hours ago, even if my face is still a little numb.' She turned to her friend. 'Thanks, Cath.'

'I'll leave you two now to have a good old gossip,' Catherine said, picking up her bag. 'I'll ring you in a couple of days. 'Bye, Lauren.'

* * *

'You look so well,' Lauren exclaimed, as they walked back inside after waving Catherine off. 'You've put on weight. It suits you. You were really thin the last time I saw you.'

'I'm a different person now. I love this climate. No more freezing cold, dismal days.'

'You have a beautiful flat, too,' Lauren said.

'I know. I'm really lucky, in so many ways. Now, tell me all about your journey.'

The two young women sat and chatted, reminiscing about old times until Anna said, 'I've made a salad. We could eat that and then go for a walk, if you'd like. It'll be cooler then. I expect you'll want an early night. It'll take you a few days to get used to the time difference.'

'Yes, I am quite tired, but I'd love to have a walk. I feel as though I've been sitting down for ever, after that long flight!'

As they were eating their salad, Lauren said, 'You told me there was someone you wanted me to meet. Was that Catherine?'

'No . . . I . . . er . . . I did want you to meet Catherine but that wasn't who I meant,' Anna blushed.

Lauren laughed. 'You've a new boyfriend. Is that right?'

'Yes. I think so.'

'What do you mean?'

'Well, I haven't known him very long. Oh, Lauren, I've never met anyone like him before. He's stunningly good looking. I don't know what he sees in me, but we've been out a few times.'

'Don't put yourself down, Anna. You're very attractive. And I'm so glad for you. You deserve someone nice after Rob. So tell me all about him.'

'Well, his name's Glenn. He's in his mid-thirties, tall, dark and handsome. I hope you'll be able to meet him while you're here. He's away in England at the moment but should be back any day now.'

'What does he do?'

'His father owns several hotels, and Glenn seems to spend his time going round visiting them, keeping his eye on things, I suppose.'

'So what's he doing in England? Is he English?'

'No. He comes from New York. He has a wonderful American accent,' Anna said. 'I think his father owns some English hotels, too.'

'Sounds interesting. I hope I'll be able to meet him. When did he leave for England?'

'Last week.'

'Have you heard from him since he's been gone?'

'Yes, a few days ago, but he wasn't sure when he would be back. He's really special, Lauren. I just keep wondering why he seems interested in me when there are so many more glamorous girls around here he could have chosen. I'm just worried that it won't last. I couldn't bear to have another broken romance so soon after my disastrous engagement,' Anna sighed.

'I'm sure that won't happen.'

'You haven't seen him. He's every girl's dream man!'

'You have got it badly,' Lauren laughed. 'This Glenn must be quite something!'

'Do you think I'm still on the rebound from Rob? And that's why I've fallen so quickly for Glenn?'

'I shouldn't think so. It was a while ago now. And what Rob did was unforgivable.'

'If only he'd explained why he left me for someone else, I'd have tried to understand,' Anna said wistfully, 'but he didn't.'

'Forget Rob. Concentrate on Glenn. If he's that stunning, it's not surprising you've fallen for him. Enjoy what you have. It's more than a year since you split up with Rob. Time to move on.'

'Yes, you're right. And I'm sorry, Lauren, but all we've done is talk about my love life. So now you tell me about yours.'

'That won't take long,' Lauren smiled, 'since my love life is non-existent.'

'I can't believe that. With your looks, there must be dozens queuing up for your attention.'

'None that I'm interested in,' she replied, trying to ignore the picture which had come into her head, of the man with the deep blue eyes she had met on the plane.

'Maybe you're still pining for Jake,' Anna said.

'That was years ago, Anna. I hardly give him a thought now.'

'No, but I think it's made you very wary of men.'

'Aren't you, after what Rob did?'

'Well, I was until I met Glenn, but now everything's changed.'

'I'm glad,' Lauren said.

* * *

The two friends ambled slowly around the attractive housing estate where Anna lived, chatting non-stop, catching up on all the news. Lauren was busy admiring the exotic plants and trees, which were in abundance, trying to learn and remember their names.

'I've only lived here a year. I don't know all their names,' Anna smiled after yet another enquiry. 'I thought we could go to the beach tomorrow morning and maybe Bay Street for shopping in the afternoon. How does that sound?'

'Wonderful, but I think I need an early night now. Jet lag's catching up with me.'

They made their way back to Anna's apartment. 'I forgot to take my cell phone out,' Anna exclaimed. 'I'll see if I have any messages.'

'Cell phone,' Lauren laughed. 'You're quite Americanised!'

'All right, mobile phone to you.'

She picked it up and said, 'Good. There's a text from Glenn.'

'From England?'

'No,' Anna squeaked, her face going pink. 'He's here. Glenn's back in Nassau and is coming round tonight!' Anna looked at her watch. 'In fact he should be here very soon. It's a good thing we came back when we did. Oh, I do so want you to meet him, Lauren.'

'Well, I'll just stay so you can introduce us, and then I'll go and have a shower and an early night. Let you two have some time together.'

'You won't mind if I go and freshen up now, will you?' Anna asked.

'No, of course not. You make yourself beautiful for Glenn. I'll unpack my things.'

'Oh, I wasn't expecting this tonight. I'm not prepared. Oh Lauren,' Anna said, clutching her friend's hand, 'supposing he's met somebody else in England. He might have found some glamorous blonde and he's coming round to tell me it's all over. I couldn't bear that.'

'Don't be silly,' Lauren said. 'He's not Rob, remember. And he wants to see you.'

'Do you really think so?'

'Yes. Now go and get changed.'

Twenty minutes later the doorbell rang. Lauren discreetly stayed in the lounge while Anna opened the door.

Lauren could hear her friend talking excitedly and then she heard a deep American voice. I must be imagining things, she thought. It's the accent. It's reminding me of . . .

The lounge door opened and Anna walked in holding the hand of a tall man. 'Lauren, this is Glenn.'

A rich American voice drawled, 'Pleased to meet . . . ' then stopped abruptly. Catching his breath, he stared down at Lauren, astonishment written all over his face.

She gasped and looked straight into the deep blue eyes of the man she had met at the airport and on the plane.

The Mystery Man

This can't be happening, Lauren thought, as Glenn let go of Anna's hand and walked towards her. The man I've been dreaming about, and who I believed would never see again, is Anna's new boyfriend. What a terrible coincidence! She tried to pull herself together, but couldn't take her eyes off Glenn as she held out her hand, wondering how to act. Should she behave as if they had just met? She didn't know what to do, but Glenn took control of the situation.

'We meet once more,' he said, gripping her hand firmly, still holding her gaze.

Lauren murmured, 'er . . . yes,' Then she blinked and pulled her hand away from him, suddenly aware that Anna was staring at them, a bemused look on her face. 'You two know each other?' she queried.

'We met at the airport and were on the same plane,' Glenn explained. He put his arm around Anna, smiled, pointed to Lauren and said, 'This woman here, trod on me in the Duty Free shop and then fell flat at my feet in the plane.'

'She what?' Anna exclaimed, looking more bewildered than ever.

'You had left your bag sticking out,' Lauren said defensively to Glenn.

'Okay. It was all my fault,' he replied gallantly. 'So, you're Anna's friend. Well, what a surprise!'

'Isn't it?' Lauren murmured half to herself.

'Anyway, now we can meet properly.' Glenn smiled again. 'How are you doing, Lauren?'

'I'm very well thanks,' she replied, still feeling somewhat disconcerted. Then, remembering her manners, she added, 'I'm pleased to meet you, Glenn.'

'How's your head?' he asked.

'Fine. How's your foot?'
'It'll survive.'
Glenn turned to Anna, who was staring at them both. He thrust a small package into her hand and said, 'Now the introductions are over, here's a little gift for you, Anna.'
'Thank you.' She pulled the bottle of perfume from its wrapper and exclaimed delightedly, 'My favourite, Glenn. How did you know?'
'I've got to be honest. You'll have to thank Lauren. She helped me choose it when we collided at the airport.'
'Oh, I see.' Anna looked from one to the other.
'I think I'll leave you two alone now,' Lauren said. 'I can't keep awake much longer.'
Truth to tell, she was glad of an excuse to escape. She was trying hard to quell the feelings of jealousy which were welling up inside her.
'You must be tired, too,' she heard Anna saying to Glenn, 'if you and Lauren were on the same flight.'

'I managed to sleep some of the time in spite of the interruptions,' he said, and winked at Lauren.

'Right. Well, goodnight then,' Lauren said, hurrying from the room, her cheeks flushed.

When she got to her room, she had a quick shower, put on a thin silk dressing gown and lay down on top of the bed, enjoying the cool breeze from the air conditioning unit. I was right about that man, she thought. He was spoken for. But by my friend! I hadn't banked on that.

I'm glad Anna has a new boyfriend. But why did it have to be him? The only man I've felt attracted to in ages! Anybody else and I'd have been rejoicing with her, but I don't fancy spending the next two weeks watching them together. Oh, grow up, she told herself. You're not twelve years old! And you don't even know him, so forget about him and enjoy your holiday.

The next morning Lauren woke at

eight, feeling refreshed. The air conditioning had kept her cool during the night and she had slept well. She had decided to throw herself into the spirit of the holiday and enjoy everything that was on offer. She would stifle the attraction she felt for Glen and be glad of Anna's good fortune. She had intended this to be a holiday of a lifetime and she wasn't going to let anything or anyone spoil it.

* * *

Anna was already up, preparing breakfast.

Lauren sat down, drank a glass of ice-cold orange juice and poured some cereal into a bowl.

'Do you feel up to walking along Bay Street this morning in downtown Nassau?' Anna asked. 'I think it might be better to do that first and leave the beach till this afternoon.'

'Sounds good. Bay Street, that's the main shopping street, isn't it?'

'Yes, and there are other areas we can visit another time. I'll show you the Straw Market today. We'll walk round it. That'll be quite an experience.'

'What do you mean?'

'I won't say any more now.' Anna smiled. 'I'll let you see for yourself.'

'Sounds interesting.'

'We could go on a horse-drawn carriage, too, if you'd like?'

'Lovely.'

'That's the good thing about having visitors. I can do all the touristy things that I don't usually have time for.'

'Haven't you been all over Nassau?' Lauren asked.

'When I first arrived, I did, but I've been too busy since. Nassau is the capital. The whole island is called New Providence.'

'How big is the island?'

'About twenty-one miles from east to west and seven miles north to south.'

'I can't wait to explore it.'

'We'll have lunch at a restaurant I know near the harbour, where you can try some of the local sea food, if you would like that?'

'Today I'm game for anything.' Lauren smiled. Then she added, 'What about your boyfriend?'

'Glenn? He's working. He might call round tonight but he wants to take us to a Junkanoo restaurant tomorrow.'

'What's that?'

'Every year there's a parade on Boxing Day and New Year's Day when people march around the streets dressed in all sorts of outrageous costumes and masks.'

'But it's not Christmas or the New Year now.'

'No, but in this restaurant people dress up in Junkanoo costumes all the year round and parade around the tables. I'll get Glenn to tell you. He knows more about it than I do.' Anna took their dishes into the kitchen. 'Let's go and tackle Bay Street if you're ready?'

Thirty minutes later they were wending their way towards the capital when Anna remarked, 'Look at that sky. I think we're in for a storm.'

Lauren had been noticing how quickly the sky had become full of clouds. 'Oh, I hope not.'

'Don't worry. We'll have a lot of those while you're here. It's the time of year.'

'Do they last long?'

'No, not usually.' Anna glanced out of the car window. 'I think I'll park here till it passes over.'

'I've never seen the weather change so fast before,' Lauren said, as they sat in the car and watched the small pitter-patter of rain drops turn into a battering torrent.

'It's because it's an island. You'll soon get used to it. Watch the clouds. You'll see them going out across the sea in a few minutes.'

Anna was right. Fifteen minutes later the storm had died away. The sun was streaming down again and the wet roads were covered in steam as they dried out.

* * *

Lauren and Anna spent the next few hours sightseeing and rummaging about in the colourful shops. They took photos in the main tourist area of Rawson Square and visited the octagonal library, which had once been the town jail. After a cooling drink, they got a horse-drawn carriage at the square and toured around old Nassau listening to a running commentary on the history of the town.

'That was a very enjoyable morning,' Lauren remarked as they were sitting in a restaurant near the harbour waiting for the conch chowder, which Anna had persuaded Lauren to try. 'I loved the Straw Market.'

'I thought you might. And I had trouble, too, when I first came here, like you did, trying to escape from all those women who want to braid your hair. They know me now so they don't bother any more.'

'And so many people trying to sell

you things that you don't want or need. It was hard to get away from them,' Laura laughed.

'I told you going there would be quite an experience. Now, we'll have a nice lazy time after lunch and just lie on the beach, if you like.'

'I can't wait. Do you go very often?'

'Not really. I did at first, but I've been too busy recently, what with writing reports, parents' meetings, not to mention all the other work that goes with being a teacher. I did manage to go at Christmas and in the Easter holiday, though.'

'So you haven't been with Glenn, then?' Lauren couldn't help asking.

'No. I don't even know if he likes sunbathing. I told you, I haven't been going out with him all that long, and he's a very busy man, travelling around a lot of the time. I keep wondering why he isn't already married.'

'It's probably because he does so much travelling. He hasn't had time to settle down.'

'Maybe,' Anna replied. 'You don't think he has been married, do you, and not told me? You've seen how gorgeous he is. You do think he's attractive?'

'Yes,' Lauren answered, thinking, he's more than just attractive, he's stunning. Then she added, 'but I don't know if he's been married. Why don't you ask him?'

'Do you think I should?'

'At least then you would know.'

'I suppose so, but we haven't talked about things like that yet.'

'Perhaps now is the time. Anyway, would it make any difference to you if he had been married? After all, you've been engaged. And he could be a widower.'

'Or divorced,' Anna added, then remarked, 'It was strange, Lauren, you meeting Glenn on the plane like that, wasn't it?'

'Yes, very,' Lauren murmured, not wanting to continue with this line of conversation.

Anna looked up. 'I think our lunch is

coming. I'm sorry, Lauren, for burdening you with my problems again. I didn't invite you here just to discuss my relationship with Glenn.'

'That's okay,' Lauren said with relief.

* * *

That evening they were relaxing in the lounge, watching television, after spending the afternoon sunbathing, paddling and swimming on Cable Beach. Lauren had thoroughly enjoyed herself. 'I think I could get used to this way of life,' she remarked.

'Well, you could always come and live out here, too.'

'It wouldn't be as easy for me as it was for you. Teachers are always in demand. I just do an ordinary secretarial job.'

'I could make enquiries for you?'

'No. I don't want to leave Michael. I think my dear brother would be horrified if I told him I was emigrating to the Bahamas. I know he'd miss me.

I'd certainly miss him if he went to live abroad. We only have each other now.'

Later that evening Glenn rang Anna to say that he was needed at one of the hotels, so he wouldn't be able to see her. Lauren noticed the look of disappointment on her friend's face as she passed on the news. 'But he will definitely be taking us to the Junkanoo restaurant tomorrow,' she said.

Lauren had ambivalent feelings. She felt sorry for Anna but in a way was relieved that she wouldn't have to watch the two of them together. She wondered if she could get out of going with them the next day.

'Do you think he really has to work?' Anna asked.

'If that's what he said. Why do you doubt him?'

'I don't know, but he has seemed strange since he's been back. Not quite like his old self. Oh,' she sighed, 'perhaps I'm imagining it.'

'But you've only seen him for a short

time and he was probably jet-lagged last night,' Lauren tried to reassure her friend.

'I expect you're right. Sorry, I do keep going on about him, don't I?'

'Look, why don't you go out with him on your own tomorrow?' Lauren said. 'I can amuse myself here.'

'I wouldn't dream of leaving you all on your own,' Anna replied. 'Besides, we're going to show you the Junkanoo restaurant. You'll love it. So no more arguments!'

* * *

The next evening they were both ready when Glenn arrived in his car to take them to the restaurant. Lauren stood in the background watching as Anna flung her arms around him and kissed him. After a few moments he disentangled himself and called, 'Hi Lauren, it's good to see you again. You're going to have a great time this evening.'

'I hope so, but if you two want to go on your own, I don't mind staying here.'

'Of course you can't do that,' Glenn answered, looking her up and down. 'Besides, you're all dressed up. We want to show you the sights of Nassau, don't we Anna?'

'I've already told her that.'

'All right. I'll say no more.'

They got into Glenn's spacious car. Anna sat in the front and Lauren stretched out in the back on the leather seats, luxuriating in the air-conditioned interior. Anna chatted excitedly to Glenn while Lauren tried not to watch. She kept forcing herself to look out of the window, telling herself that she wanted to see the scenery, but her eyes seemed drawn as if by a magnet to Glenn.

She was admiring his thick brown hair and the way it curled around the nape of his neck, when she caught him glancing at her in the driving mirror. She turned away quickly and stared out of the window. You have got to stop this, she told herself. He's Anna's friend. She'll notice if you keep gazing at him. You're going to be here for quite a few more days yet, and will see the two of them together several times, so you'd better get used to it, and feel pleased for Anna that she's found someone so nice.

'What do you think, Lauren?'

She was startled by Glenn's question.

'I'm sorry?' she stammered. 'What do I think about what?' She'd been so wrapped up in her thoughts, she hadn't heard the question.

Glenn laughed. 'Are you falling asleep in the back? We haven't got far to go. I'll keep quiet and let you rest, if that's what you want.'

'No. I'm not asleep, I . . . I . . .'

Anna turned round to look at her friend. 'Are you all right, Lauren? You're not usually this quiet.'

'I'm okay. I was just looking out of the window at the scenery,' Lauren replied.

* * *

When they arrived at the restaurant, there were a lot of people wandering around, both tourists and locals. 'I hope we can get a table,' Anna said.

'We will,' Glenn said. 'They know me in there. They'll always find room for us.'

'You seem to know everyone,' Anna laughed, catching hold of his hand and gazing up at him.

They went inside and, sure enough, were soon ushered to a table. After they had perused the menu and made their choices, Lauren asked, 'Are you going to tell me all about Junkanoo? It's a fascinating name.'

'It is,' Glenn replied. 'There are different theories as to its origins. One says that it comes from the name John Canoe. He was a mythical African chief who was brought to the West Indies as a slave, but demanded that his captors should let him and his fellow slaves have the right to continue

their own celebrations.'

'Oh, now I understand. This restaurant is called Johnny Canoe, or Junkanoo.'

'But that's only one theory,' Glenn said.

'Isn't there another idea that it was started by some slaves?' Anna broke in.

'Yes. That's right. At Christmas time, slaves were given three days off, and to celebrate this they dressed up, wore masks, danced about and played home-made musical instruments like goatskin drums and cowbells,' Glenn told them, and then added, 'their music is called Goombay.'

'You'll see the dancers soon. They parade through the restaurant. I've been here once before,' Anna confided.

'I didn't know,' Glenn replied. 'You never said.'

'I never thought to say. We came from school to celebrate someone's birthday a few months ago. I thoroughly enjoyed it and the food was good too.'

'And I thought I was giving you a new experience!' Glenn said.

* * *

Soon they were enjoying a traditional Bahamian meal of fried chicken, peas and rice and coleslaw. They were nearly finished when the dancers started their parade through the restaurant. They got up from their seats to see better and Lauren took several photographs. Glenn used his digital camera and promised to print the photos off for them. It was an entertaining evening and they were all sorry when it was time to leave.

Glenn drove them back to Anna's flat. She invited him in but he declined, saying that he had to be at work early in the morning. When they reached the door, Lauren called, 'Goodnight Glenn, thanks for a lovely evening,' and hurried inside. She didn't want to witness the two of them kissing each other.

'Don't you like Glenn?' Anna asked, when she eventually came inside.

'Of course I do. Why do you ask?'

'I'm not sure, but you seemed a bit

reserved with him.'

'I was just a bit tired. I think I'll get ready for bed now. Goodnight, Anna, I've really enjoyed today. Thank you.'

The next day, Anna and Lauren got up late and spent a lot of time lazing on the beach and swimming.

In the evening, while they were eating their dinner, Anna's phone rang. 'I wonder who that can be,' she said as she went to pick up the receiver. 'Most people ring my cell phone these days.

'Hello,' she answered. 'Anna Jackson here.'

A few moments later Lauren heard her gasp and exclaim, 'Oh no. I'll come as soon as I can. I'll ring you back when I've made arrangements.'

'Whatever is it?' Lauren asked, noting her friend's pale face.

'It's my dad. He's been taken ill. He's in hospital. He needs a heart operation. I'll have to go back to England.'

An Alarming Event

'I'm so sorry, Anna,' Lauren said. 'Look, I'll travel back with you. Let's ring the airport now and book a flight.' She put her arm around her friend.

'No. You must stay here. I don't want to cut short your holiday.'

'That's all right. I can't let you travel back on your own.'

'Don't be silly,' Anna said, 'I'm quite capable of travelling on my own.'

'I know that, but I thought you might like the company. Besides, there's no point in my staying here without you. I came here to be with you.

'Look, why don't you ring your mother back and find out some more details? I'll look on the web and find out which flights are available.'

'Thanks, Lauren, I think I will phone Mum, but I've had an idea.. I'll tell you about it when I've spoken to her.'

'Okay. I'll check the flight times while you're doing that.'

Lauren busied herself on the computer while her friend spoke to her mother.

A few minutes later Anna said, 'My dad should be having his operation in two days, if he continues to make good progress. Apparently he became ill at work last week and was sent home, but he didn't see a doctor. He thought he'd be better in a few days. That's so typical of him. He doesn't like making a fuss. But this morning he took a turn for the worse and Mum called the doctor. He sent for an ambulance and Dad was rushed straight into hospital.'

'Was it a heart attack?'

'I don't think so, but he needs an operation, a valve replacement, they said. They're trying to stabilise him so he'll be fit enough for it.'

'He hasn't had any problems before, has he?'

'No, not that I know of.'

'Well, I'm sure he'll be all right.

Doctors can do marvellous things these days,' Lauren tried to reassure her friend.

'Yes, and Mum says he's quite cheerful. He didn't want her to tell me. He said there was no need for me to come back to England, but Mum thought I would want to know. And I'll feel happier if I go and see him for myself.' Anna sighed. 'He was supposed to be coming out to Nassau with Mum for Christmas. He's retiring in December. And he's been so looking forward to coming.'

'He might still be able to.'

'Yes, of course.'

'I've looked up some flights for us,' Lauren said.

'No, Lauren. I'll go on my own. I'm not going to ruin your holiday. And my idea is that Catherine will keep an eye on you. I'm sure Glenn will look in on you, too, if I ask him.'

'You can't impose me on to them!'

'They won't mind. I was going to suggest that Catherine came out with us some of the time, anyway. And it might only be for a few days. I'll phone Glenn. I'll see what he has to say.'

'No!' Lauren shrieked. She didn't want to be left on her own with him. She was far too attracted to him.

Anna stared at her. 'I was right. You don't like him, do you?'

Lauren felt herself blushing. 'Of course I do.' Too much, she thought to herself. 'It's just that I don't want to inflict myself on anyone. Besides, if you insist that I stay, there's plenty I can do here on my own. Sunbathing, swimming, shopping, for example.'

'Well, if you're sure. But Glenn would have been good company for you.'

They spent the next twenty minutes sorting out which would be the best flight for Anna. She phoned the airport and booked it for the next afternoon. After getting in touch with her mother again, she settled down for a long conversation with Glenn. Lauren kept out of her way and sat down in the kitchen to write some postcards she had bought the day before.

When Anna had finished, she joined Lauren, sitting opposite her at the table. 'I'll talk to Catherine in the morning,' she told her. 'Glenn's taking some time off so he can take me to the airport. You can come with us.'

'You won't want me tagging along.'

'Don't be silly. You won't be tagging along, as you put it.'

'Of course I will. He's your boyfriend. He'll want you to himself, especially as he won't be seeing you for a few days. Three's a crowd, remember?'

'Glenn travels around a lot, so we often don't meet for days.'

'All the more reason why I'm not coming. Make the most of your time with him.'

'I still think you're trying to avoid him,' Anna said, 'but I'm not going to get into an argument.'

'Good.'

The next day Lauren was sitting

drinking coffee. Anna was packed and ready to go. She had telephoned her mother and had been pleased to hear that her father was in a stable condition. 'He should be having his operation in the morning,' she told Lauren. 'Dad says there's no need for me to come, but I can't rest until I've seen him for myself. If all goes well, I won't be gone too long. I'm so sorry I've spoilt your holiday, Lauren.'

'Don't you worry about me. I'll amuse myself.'

'Catherine's coming over later, and I'm sure Glenn will help out, too, no matter what you say,' Anna reassured her. 'Oh, that sounds like him now.'

She opened the door while Lauren felt her heart beating faster as she heard the now familiar voice.

'Hi Lauren,' Glenn said, as he came in. 'It's too bad what's happened to Anna's Dad, but I believe Catherine's going to be looking after you for the next few days while Anna's away?'

'Yes, that's right.'

'But you'll take Lauren out too, won't you?' Anna said.

'Well, I'm not sure what time I'll have,' Glenn answered, looking at Lauren.

'Don't fret about me,' she replied, looking away thinking, he doesn't want to have to be bothered with me.

Don't feel so disappointed, she chided herself. It's better this way.

'But I will worry about you,' she heard him saying. 'I'll feel responsible for you while Anna's away in England, but unfortunately it's my really busy time. It's the vacation season as you know, and several staff are away, so I'm having to go from hotel to hotel filling in for them.'

'That's a shame,' Anna interjected.

'Look,' Lauren said, 'I'm a big girl now, so there's no need for everyone to fuss over me. I'm quite capable of fending for myself. Anna, you go back to England for as long as you need.' She turned to Glenn, 'and you can get on with your work with a clear conscience.

I'll be perfectly happy.'

'If you say so,' he said.

Several minutes later Glenn and Anna had left for the airport. Lauren was busy preparing a salad for her lunch when Catherine called round. 'I'm taking you to the beach this afternoon, and then we'll go out to dinner,' she said. 'I know just the place, good food, not too expensive and you can meet my fiancé.'

'Are you sure you can spare the time?' Lauren said.

'Of course. It's the summer holiday. I've plenty of time. Besides, it gives me an excuse to do some sunbathing!'

* * *

For the next three days, Catherine and Lauren spent a lot of time together, both liking the other's company. Considering the disastrous start to her holiday, Lauren found she was thoroughly enjoying herself. Catherine and her fiancé, Peter, had gone out of their way to make her stay pleasurable. Peter was tall, good looking, and friendly, and made Lauren feel very welcome, and not like an outsider. His family were native Bahamians, coming from Cat Island, where Peter had been born. He had moved to Nassau, seeking work in the travel industry. He, too, like Glenn, worked in the hotel business, but as a manager based at one particular hotel.

Lauren was surprised she didn't feel as if she were intruding when she was with Catherine and Peter. Yet she'd felt in the way when she'd been with Anna and Glenn, even though they had tried to assure her that she wasn't. I suppose it's because Catherine and Peter's relationship is more secure, she mused, whereas Anna and Glenn are still getting to know each other. Or perhaps it's all in my mind, she thought; maybe it's my awkwardness at finding Glenn so attractive. But there was one thing that she was relieved about. She hadn't heard from Glenn. She wouldn't have known how to handle that.

* * *

Anna phoned Lauren and told her that her father was doing well after his operation. 'The doctors expect him to make a full recovery,' she informed her, 'so I'll probably get a flight back at the weekend.. So, what have you been doing? I hope you've been well looked after.'

Lauren talked enthusiastically about the places she had visited with Catherine and Peter.

'Haven't you seen Glenn?' Anna asked. 'I've only managed to speak to him for a short time, since I've been away. He always seems to be busy.'

'I haven't seen him, no, but you know I told him there was no need to worry about me.'

'I'm going to ring him in a minute to find out what's going on. At least he could have rung you.'

'Please don't fuss over me, Anna. Honestly, I've had a really good time.'

'All right, if you're sure.'

'Perfectly.'

That evening, while Lauren was getting ready to go out for a meal with Catherine and Peter, the doorbell rang. She quickly threw on a wrap and flew across the hallway, expecting to see Catherine. She flung the door open, then gasped as she realised it was Glenn who was standing there.

'Hi,' he said, eyeing her up and down. 'I'm sorry I've caught you at a bad time. I thought I'd better look in on you to see how you were doing.'

Lauren caught her breath as she gazed up into Glenn's deep blue eyes. He reached for her hand and smiled down at her.

'I'm . . . er . . . fine,' she stammered, still clutching his hand, noting his immaculate appearance, his pristine white shirt and expensive-looking suit. She blushed, feeling embarrassed at being in her tatty old robe. She quickly pulled her hand away and said, 'Will you excuse me while I get ready? Catherine and Peter will be here any minute. Go and sit in the lounge. I won't be long. Pour yourself a drink. There's plenty in the fridge.'

'OK. Thanks. Where are you and Catherine going?' he called after Lauren as she disappeared into the bedroom, firmly closing the door behind her.

'I don't know,' she called back, sitting on the bed. Oh, why did he have to come now? He had the ability to make her feel like a silly schoolgirl, yet she had no right to feel this way. He's Anna's friend she once again reminded herself, as she hurried to get ready.

Ten minutes later Lauren came back into the lounge where Glenn was sitting on the sofa reading the local newspaper and sipping a fruit juice. He looked up and she noted the way he was studying her appearance.

'Now, tell me what you've been doing,' he said.

She was about to do so when Catherine arrived. 'Hello, you two, nice to see you again, Glenn. Sorry I'm on my own, but Peter's been called into work, some sort of emergency.'

'I know the feeling,' Glenn murmured. 'That's why I haven't been around this week. Too much to do and not enough time to do it. Now I know why my dad's looking forward to his retirement. This hotel business takes over your life,' he sighed.

'That's what Peter says, and he only works in the Bahamas. He's not an international jet-setter like you, buying hotels all over the world!'

'Not quite,' Glenn smiled. 'Just New York, Washington, London, Glasgow, Edinburgh, and here in Cable Beach.'

'I should think that's enough,' Catherine laughed. 'Look, if you're not too busy, would you like to come out with us tonight?'

'I'd love to, if that's all right with Lauren.' He looked expectantly at her. 'Well, is it OK if I come, too?' he repeated.

'Oh, of course,' she replied politely, thinking, why did Catherine have to ask him?

'Where are we going then?' he asked.

'I thought we'd drive along the coast, see all the hotels lit up at night, and then have dinner at a little place I know overlooking the sea. I often go there with Peter.'

'Sounds delightful,' Glenn said. He turned to Lauren. 'Some time before you go home, you'll have to have dinner at one of my hotels. I'll arrange it for you, and if I'm not around, I'll get someone to look after you.'

'Thank you,' she murmured, thinking it would be better if someone else did look after her.

'Are we all ready?' Catherine said. 'Then let's go.'

As they walked to her car, Glenn asked Lauren, 'Have you been to Paradise Island yet?'

'No, but Anna said she would take me there when she comes back, and to Discovery Island, too, and the place where you can swim with the dolphins. That's if there's enough time left before I have to go back.'

'You're sure going to be kept busy.'

* * *

They drove along beside the sea. Lauren sat in the front next to Catherine. She was trying to take everything in, so that when she returned to England she would be able to relive these memories. She wanted to remember how the sun set over the sea in a gold and red haze, and how bright lights in all the colours of the rainbow streamed from the hotels as the tourists strutted up and down in their finery. Glenn sat in the back saying nothing. She wondered if he was missing Anna.

They ended up in a little restaurant overlooking a secluded cove.

'You must try the conch,' Catherine said, 'and what about a Bahamian cocktail? Will you have one, Lauren?'

'Please. It sounds lovely. I'll try whatever you recommend.'

The food was delicious and Lauren sat back and relaxed. Catherine and Glenn did most of the talking. Lauren was content just to sit and listen. They were mainly talking about the hotel industry.

'My father's hoping to buy another hotel on Paradise Island,' Glenn told them, 'so I'm going to be busy negotiating that in the next few weeks, as well as filling in as manager when staff are away on vacation. My dad's winding down now, but he's the one who gets the ideas and then expects me to carry them out. That's why Anna never knows when she's going to see me,' he explained to Lauren. 'I'm forever having to go around looking for any potential acquisitions. My dad wants to keep adding to his chain.'

'Oh, I see,' Lauren said.

'I hope we haven't bored you with all this talk about hotels, Lauren,' Catherine said.

'No, of course not. It's a whole new world to me, and I find it fascinating.'

'Good. Now it's your turn to talk. Tell us about your job,' Glenn said.

'There's nothing to tell. My life in England is very boring and dull compared to yours here.'

'I'm sure it's not,' Glenn replied. 'What do you do?'

'I'm just a secretary. I work in a little office in London.'

'I love London,' Glenn said. 'There's so much to do and see. Don't you agree, Catherine?'

'Yes. I used to look forward to my shopping trips to Oxford Street when I lived in Kent.'

Glenn laughed. 'A typical female remark! I wasn't referring to the shops. I was thinking about all the historic buildings, the river, the theatres. It's so different from New York, where I come from. More modern in some ways, but full of tradition in others.'

'I'd love to see New York,' Lauren said. 'Have you been there?' she asked Catherine.

'No, but I'm hoping to go there with Peter after we're married. Glenn's told us we can use his apartment while he's away.'

'Yeah, that's right. I seem to spend

more time travelling around than I do at home, which reminds me, delightful as this evening has been, I think I should head back to my hotel, if you don't mind, Catherine. I've got an early start in the morning. I'm off to Washington.'

'You do get around,' Catherine laughed.

I probably won't see him any more, Lauren thought. By the time he gets back, I'll be in England.

'I hope to see you again before you go home,' Glenn was saying, as if he was reading her thoughts.

She noted his piercing blue eyes gazing into hers and quickly looked away. 'Yes, I hope so too,' she murmured. 'Anna should be back in a day or two. She'll miss you.'

'I'll see her soon enough.'

Half an hour later, Catherine was driving them back. She stopped at a petrol station.

'I can get out here,' Glenn told her. 'It's only a couple of minutes' walk to my hotel.'

'Okay. Have a safe journey. See you soon.' She turned to Lauren. 'I won't be long.' She got out of the car and walked over to the petrol pump.

Lauren had been sitting in the front of the car. She glanced around, expecting to see Glenn getting out the back, but he was still sitting there, looking at her intently. She was embarrassed to find herself blushing.

'Goodnight, Lauren. Enjoy the rest of your holiday. I'm sorry I have to leave.'

'That can't be helped,' she replied, thinking, it's probably better that he is going.

'I'll try very hard to get back to Nassau before you leave.'

'Anna will be pleased.'

'Will she?'

'Of course. Have a . . . ' But before she could say any more, he'd stepped out of the car and was heading off up the road.

* * *

That night Lauren couldn't sleep. She tossed and turned, reliving the events of the evening. Her main thought was the realisation that she had fallen in love with her best friend's boyfriend. How could she have done that? She hardly knew the man. Yet she knew that this wasn't just a passing infatuation. She'd never felt this way about anyone before, not even Jake. All those years ago she'd thought she loved him, but it wasn't like this feeling she had for Glenn.

But it was all wrong, she couldn't do this. Nothing could ever come of it. Glenn loved Anna, and Lauren was sure that Anna loved him, but he didn't seem to know that. Was it because Anna was still unsure of herself after what her fiancé had done?

Anyone would feel insecure, if they discovered that the man they were going to marry was having an affair with one of their friends. That was what Rob had done. When Anna found out, she told him their engagement was off. He begged and pleaded with her to forgive him, and promised that the affair was over and he would never do anything like that again, but Anna was too distraught to listen and told him she never wanted to see him again.

Finding a teaching post in the Bahamas seemed the best thing that could have happened to Anna in the circumstances, Lauren mused.

She thought back over her past life. Like Anna, she had been deceived, too. Jake, her first love, had been unfaithful to her, and it had taken years to get over it. Now she knew that she had no feelings left for him, but she was racked with guilt for being so attracted to Glenn, even though nothing improper had passed between them.

She'd go back to England and try to forget Glenn. It would be hard but she would have to do it for her friend's sake. It would be better if he didn't return from Washington until after she had gone home. Now that she had acknowledged to herself her feelings for him, seeing him again would be too painful. She remembered how he had looked at her as he said goodbye. Did that mean anything? Or had she just imagined there was some hidden meaning in it? Anyway, even if there was, nothing could come from it. He belonged to Anna.

Lauren drifted in and out of sleep, half aware of the wind howling outside and the rain which was beating down, until suddenly she was startled by the telephone ringing. She glanced at her watch. It was four o'clock. Whoever could be ringing at this hour? Then her heart sank. It must be Anna, she thought. She must have bad news. Lauren picked up the receiver and murmured, 'Hello?'

'Hi there. It's Glenn.' As if she could ever mistake his voice, she thought.

'I'm sorry if I've woken you up. You do sound sleepy, but I've just heard the weather forecast. We're in for a tropical storm.'

'Oh no.' She'd read about them but had hoped never to experience one.

'The weather men had predicted that it would bypass the Bahamas but the wind has changed and they think it will affect us tomorrow. It could be a bad one. I've phoned the airport and found out that my flight to Washington has been cancelled, as have all the other flights out of Nassau.'

'What should I do?' Lauren asked in alarm.

'You have to put the shutters up at the windows, and you need to get some candles ready and store plenty of water for washing and drinking. We may be without power for some time. Look, I think I'd better come over to make sure you're okay. I'll get a cab and be with you as soon as I can.'

'No,' she said. 'I'll be all right. I'll do what you said. Don't come out in this weather. I . . . I can hear the wind and rain. You'll get soaked just getting into a taxi.'

'Don't worry about me. I'm used to these conditions. You're not. I can't leave you there on your own. Anna would never forgive me.'

'But . . . but . . . '

'No buts. I'll be there as soon as I can.'

Lauren realised the line had gone dead. He'd hung up. Now what was she going to do? A tropical storm was bad enough, and Glenn was right, she didn't want to be on her own, but spending the rest of the night with him was not what she'd had in mind. She'd just resolved to put him out of her mind for good. Now she was going to be spending time on her own with him.

Lauren quickly got dressed. She busied herself pulling the shutters across and filling up jugs and kettles with water. She also filled the bath. She rummaged around the drawers in the kitchen and found some candles and matches. Anna had told her that these flats were very well built, and were designed to withstand tropical storms and earthquakes, so she should be all right.

A few minutes later the telephone

rang again. Lauren half expected it to be Glenn, but it was Catherine. 'I've just had a call from Glenn. He's told me that he'll make sure you're all right during the storm. Do you mind if I don't come over? I would have tried to get to you, but he told me not to bother, as the conditions outside are really atrocious now. He's quite confident he'll be able to get to you, though.'

'Of course I don't mind. I don't want you putting yourself at risk, and I told Glenn not to come, but he wouldn't listen.'

'Ever the gentleman. Besides, Anna would have expected him to take care of you.'

'That's what he said, but I'm quite capable of looking after myself.'

'Yes but it isn't very nice being alone in a strange place in a tropical storm.'

'I suppose not, but I don't want to be a burden to anybody.'

'You won't be. Glenn's very practical. He'll soon get you sorted out.'

'But I'm sorted already.'

'You don't sound very keen on Glenn coming round. Don't you like him?'

'Of course I do.'

I've had this conversation with Anna, Lauren thought. Everyone thinks I don't like Glenn, when in fact it's the opposite. 'But I just don't want to be a bother,' she said again.

'You won't be. Glenn likes taking care of people. Anyway, I'd better go and get myself organised for this terrible weather. I'll try and ring you in the morning, but it's quite likely the power lines will be down by then, so I'll talk to you when I can. Take care!'

'Thank you. I hope you'll be all right. Is Peter there with you?'

'No. I told him not to try and get here. I'll be okay. I'm used to these conditions. I'll have to go. Bye Lauren.'

'Bye, and good luck.'

'Good luck to you too,' Catherine said.

I think I might need that, Lauren mused.

* * *

The telephone rang again. It was Anna, sounding alarmed. 'I was having my breakfast when I heard the forecast for the Bahamas,' she said. 'I can't believe it. I really expected the storm to bypass you. Glenn's just rung me and said he's on his way to the flat. He'll look after you.'

'I keep telling everyone that I don't need looking after, but no-one seems to listen.'

'Well, you won't want to be alone at a time like this. It's bad enough for those of us who are used to the storms. I wouldn't want to be on my own in one.'

'No, but I am prepared,' Lauren said. 'I've done what Glenn told me to do. And I have water and candles.'

'It's much better to have someone to be with, though, when it's raging outside.'

'I suppose so. And I'm sorry, Anna, with all this going on I forgot to ask about your father. How is he?'

'Making very good progress.'

'I am glad.'

'As soon as the storm's over and things have settled, I'll be back. Look after yourself, Lauren. Hope to see you soon.'

'Thanks for ringing, Anna. Bye.'

'Good luck, Lauren.'

'Thanks, Anna.' And I'm definitely going to need that, Lauren thought.

The Night Of The Storm

Lauren put the coffee maker on. Glenn will need a drink when he gets here after braving the storm, she thought, and I do too. I'd better find some towels for him to dry himself off, too.

She was just putting fresh towels in the bathroom when the doorbell rang.

She hurried to the door. Glenn was standing outside, dripping from head to foot. 'Hi. Can you pass me a towel? I'll try not to drip all over Anna's flat.'

Lauren rushed into the bathroom, grabbed a towel and flew back to him.

'It's okay,' he said. 'I can wait a minute. I won't die from exposure, but you might collapse from lack of breath if you don't take it easy.'

Lauren realised that she was indeed gasping for breath. Was it because she'd been hurrying or was it because Glenn was here looking absolutely gorgeous, despite being soaking wet?

She felt rather silly and tried to walk sedately back across the hall. 'There are some more towels in the bathroom, if you want,' she said, in what she hoped was a cool, calm, voice.

'Thanks. And I've brought some dry clothes to change into.'

'OK. While you're doing that, shall I make a coffee?'

'There's nothing I would like better. You must have read my mind,' he smiled.

Lauren went into the kitchen, got some mugs ready and started to make the coffee. She was annoyed to find that her hands were shaking.

She put the mugs on a tray, found some biscuits, placed them on a plate and carried everything into the lounge. She put the tray down on the table, glad that Glenn was not already there. It gave her a chance to compose herself before he came in. She sat down, wishing her heart would stop beating so fast.

'I feel better already,' Glenn remarked as he came in and sat down opposite Lauren. He'd changed into jeans and a T-shirt. His tousled hair made him look even more appealing, she thought.

'Gee, that coffee sure smells good,' he murmured.

'I didn't know if you were hungry. If you like, I could make you some breakfast.'

'I think five o'clock is a bit early for that,' he grinned.

'Oh . . . yes, I suppose it is.'

'These biscuits will be fine. And I've checked the shutters, Lauren. You've done a good job there.'

'Thanks.'

'You seem very calm. Have you ever been caught in a tropical storm before?'

Lauren was glad she looked calm. She certainly didn't feel it, but that wasn't because of the weather. 'No, but Anna told me what to expect and as I have a kind gentleman to protect me, why should I be worried?' she said, trying to lighten the situation.

'It's the least I can do. I feel bad enough about you being here on your own while Anna's away. I'm sorry I haven't been able to do more for you.'

'I've been quite all right, thank you.'

'Oh Lauren, you sound so English, so quaint,' he laughed.

'Well, I am English,' she answered primly.

'Do you know, that's just what Anna often says.'

'She's English too.'

'I know that only too well,' he muttered.

Now what did that mean, Lauren wondered? But she wasn't going to ask him. It was none of her business.

As Glenn drank his coffee, Lauren couldn't stop herself from looking at him, thinking that, even in these casual clothes, and with his hair damp, he was still stunning. He seemed to ooze confidence and charm. She'd never met anyone like him. Maybe it was because he was American, or because he'd spent his life travelling around the world. She felt awkward and gauche in comparison.

'I see you've got some candles ready. Good girl,' Glenn said. 'We might need them in a minute. The lights keep flickering, but at least it will be getting light soon.'

Lauren glanced up and saw that he was staring at her. She looked away, embarrassed to find herself blushing. 'Would you like another coffee?'

'That would be great. You'd better have one as well. If the power does go off, it might be some time before it comes back on again.'

She escaped to the kitchen, to hide her flaming cheeks. She poured the coffee and was just about to go back to the lounge when there was an enormous clap of thunder the like of which she had never heard before, followed by a flash of fork lightning. Then everything went dark. The shock made her drop the tray. As it crashed to the floor she couldn't stop herself from crying out as the hot coffee splashed on her leg.

Suddenly she felt strong arms around her. 'Are you okay, Lauren? Don't worry about the coffee. I'll clear it up later.'

She leaned back against Glenn, trying not to sob. Then, realising what she was doing, she straightened up. 'It's my leg. The . . . the . . . coffee splashed it.' She was glad that in the dark, he couldn't see her scarlet face. Why had she put on this short skirt? If she'd worn her jeans they would have protected her legs. She felt so stupid. Every time she saw Glenn something seemed to happen to make her feel inadequate and clumsy. But did it matter? He was Anna's boyfriend. What he thinks of me is unimportant, Lauren reminded herself.

He picked her up gently and carried her into the lounge and put her down on the sofa. Then he lit some candles and came and knelt beside her. 'I seem to be making a habit of coming to your rescue, Lauren. Let me see what you've done.' His voice was full of concern. 'We need to run some cold water over your leg,' he said, going to get a bowl from the kitchen.

Lauren tried to make herself comfortable on the sofa. She could hear the wind and rain howling outside and further claps of thunder. The lightning continued to flash, illuminating the room.

'I don't think it's too serious,' Glenn remarked when he returned, 'but it might be as well to see a doctor when this storm's over.'

'I'm sorry I'm such a nuisance,' Lauren apologised, 'but the noise of the thunder was so loud it made me jump, and then the lights going out as well, I just didn't expect that. I know you had warned me, so I should have been prepared.'

'Hush. Stop worrying,' Glenn said, as he gently poured cold water over her leg. 'You couldn't help being startled. I feel responsible. If I had come into the kitchen to help you we could have avoided this. I guess Anna will scold me for not looking after you properly.'

'But you are looking after me. Nobody could do any better,' Lauren protested, then glanced away. Those eyes! They seemed to be gazing into her soul. 'And you're not responsible for my accident,' she continued. 'I'm a grown woman and should be able to take care of myself. Anna won't tell you off. She knows I'm not a helpless little female.'

'I'm sure you're not, and in the right circumstances you're probably more than capable of looking after yourself, but you aren't used to tropical storms. I am. I've been coming over here enough years to know what they're like.' He stopped pouring water over her leg and said, 'I think that should feel more comfortable. I'm just glad I was able to get here in time, to be with you.'

'My leg does feel better, thanks. You've done a marvellous job, Doctor . . . you know, I've just realised I don't know your surname.' She was trying to lighten the situation.

'Eastwood, Glenn David Eastwood. That's me. And I'm no doctor, only a humble hotel worker.'

'You've been like a doctor to me. And from what Catherine said, you're an international jet-setter, not just a humble hotel worker.'

'Catherine exaggerates. I just travel around keeping my eye on my father's acquisitions, and helping out generally as a relief manager if required.'

'Don't you also keep a lookout for new hotels to add to your father's chain?'

'Yeah, that's right. You've a good memory. I didn't think you'd remember that.'

She'd remembered every word Glenn had said, but she wasn't going to tell him that.

'How does your leg feel now?' he asked.

'Much better, thanks.'

'You're very flushed. I hope you haven't got a temperature.'

'Well, I am rather hot. It must be because the air conditioning's gone off.'

'I think these candles are making it warmer, too. We should be able to blow them out soon. It's getting much lighter now.'

'How long do you think the storm will last?'

'I've no idea. Sometimes they go on for ages, but they can die out all of a sudden. As this one wasn't predicted, I can't tell. I keep thinking how glad I am that I left my flight until today. If I'd gone to Washington yesterday, you'd have been here on your own.'

'I would have coped.'

'No doubt, but it isn't nice being on your own in a tropical storm, especially if it's your first.' Glenn was staring at her. He took hold of her hand, lightly pressed her wrist, let go and stroked her forehead, exclaiming, 'You're burning up. Your pulse is racing. We've got to cool you down.'

'I'm okay,' she protested, but suddenly she didn't feel it. Was it Glenn's touch that had done it or was it the heat that was getting to her? 'I do feel a bit strange,' she murmured.

Glenn put his arms around her, laid her down on the sofa and placed some pillows behind her head. He hurried to the kitchen and came back with another bowl of water, which he placed on the coffee table. Then he went into the bathroom and returned with a flannel. Lauren just lay there. She felt too weak to do anything else.

'Did you go on the beach yesterday?' Glenn asked, kneeling down beside her.

'Er . . . yes . . . ' She tried to lift her head but a sharp pain shot through her. She moaned and sank back onto the cushion.

'Oh Lauren, what's wrong?' He stroked her hand gently.

'It's my . . . head. It's so . . . so . . . painful.'

Glenn sponged her face and neck. 'You've had too much sun and this heat on top of it is making you feel ill. I'll have to get you to a doctor as soon as we can go outside. I'm afraid I can't even telephone as they're not working because of the storm, and our mobiles are no use either.'

He continued to sponge her. His touch was so gentle and caring but she couldn't really appreciate it. She felt too ill.

Suddenly the room was spinning round. Lauren had to get to the bathroom. She was going to be sick. Why had she drunk that coffee? She tried to get up off the sofa, but felt too weak.

Glenn must have seen her face change and, realising what was going to happen, picked her up and carried her to the bathroom, saying, 'Call me when you feel better.'

Fifteen minutes later, she no longer felt sick, but was still very weak and light-headed. She made her way slowly back to the lounge where Glenn was sitting with his head in his hands. Surely he wasn't ill now!

'I told you to call me,' he said,

rushing to her side, scooping her up in his arms and placing her down on the sofa. 'Oh, Lauren, you've got me so worried,' he said, stroking her hair, gazing into her eyes.

What was he doing? Why was he looking at her like that? She must be delirious. 'I'm a little better now,' she murmured, wanting to pull away, but feeling too weak to resist. 'Are you all right?'

'I'm out of my mind worrying about you.'

'There's no need. I'm on the mend.' But was she? She was beginning to feel sick again.

Glenn picked her up, once more depositing her in the bathroom. 'And this time, call me when you want to come out,' he ordered.

Ten minutes later Lauren lay back against the bath trying to regain her strength. She was determined to make her own way back to the lounge. She didn't want Glenn holding her again. Her mind was beginning to play strange tricks on her and she was imagining all sorts of things that couldn't possibly be there. She forced herself up and was creeping back to the lounge when Glenn spotted her. He put his arm around her and helped her back to the sofa. 'I thought I told you to call me when you were ready.'

'I'm all right now,' she murmured.

'Well, you don't look it.'

'Thanks.'

'Look Lauren, why don't you go back to bed for a few hours? You'll feel a lot better if you have a sleep. I'll sit in here and read or something.'

That did sound like a good idea. She felt so tired and weak, her head was pounding and she needed to get away from Glenn. He was being too nice. It was going to be so much harder going back home, remembering the way he had cared for her and how safe she had felt in his arms. But he belongs to Anna, she had to keep telling herself.

'I will have a rest, if you don't mind,' she said, getting up as quickly as she could.

'Let me help you.' He was beside her again.
'No, I can manage, thank you.'
'Well, call me if you need anything.'
'All right.'

* * *

Lauren tottered into the bedroom, shut the door and lay down on the bed. She sensed that Glenn was staring after her, but didn't look back at him. She lay quietly for some time unable to sleep, feeling acutely aware that Glenn was in the next room. She felt embarrassed that she had been so ill while he was there and vowed that for the rest of her holiday she would be much more aware of the strength of the sun.

She kept remembering the way Glenn had looked at her, but then told herself that he was only treating her in the same way he would anyone who was ill. He was a kind, considerate man. It was the fever making her imagine things. Gradually she drifted off to sleep, still hearing the sound of the wind howling and the rain battering against the window.

* * *

Several hours later an enormous clap of thunder woke Lauren. It took her a few moments to come to. She sat up and realised that she felt much better. Her head was no longer aching and she didn't feel sick any more. Her leg was less painful, too. And she felt quite hungry.

She got out of bed, looked at her watch and was surprised to find that it was past eleven o'clock. She'd been asleep nearly five hours! It was still dark and gloomy because of the shutters and the electricity hadn't come back on. They still needed candles. She smoothed her clothes and, after freshening up, she went back to the lounge where Glenn was sleeping on the sofa. She tiptoed to the kitchen and had a drink of water. She would have loved a cup of tea and some toast but had to settle for a piece of bread and butter instead. She was clearing away her plate and tumbler when the kitchen door opened.

'What on earth are you doing?' Glenn said.

'Tidying up.'

'I could have done that. You should be resting.'

'I'm feeling much better now.'

'But you won't be, if you overdo it. Go and put your feet up,' he ordered.

'If you insist,' she murmured. She did feel rather weak and breathless. Was it the exertion after being so sick, or was it the nearness of Glen that was causing it? He was standing close, his arms folded, staring down at her, an unfathomable look in his eyes.

Lauren went into the lounge and stretched out on the sofa. She could hear the rain still beating down and the wind howling. Would this storm never end? She was trapped in the flat with Glenn until it did.

His presence was unsettling, making her imagination run away with her. It would be so easy to forget he was Anna's boyfriend. But that was the one thing she mustn't do.

A few minutes later Glenn came into the lounge carrying some fruit juice and a sandwich. He sat down opposite Lauren. 'I'm glad to see you're taking my advice. You need to rest, otherwise you won't be able to enjoy the rest of your vacation. Now, don't you move, if you want anything, just ask me.'

'Okay, doctor,' she smiled.

'I think it's beginning to get lighter,' Glenn said. 'Maybe the storm is passing.'

'I hope so.'

'How's your leg?'

'Much better, thank you.'

'It's a shame all this had to happen to spoil your vacation.'

'Don't worry about that. I've had a lovely holiday in spite of everything. Everyone's been so kind.'

'I'm sorry I haven't done much for

you, but I had to work.'

'You've been marvellous. No-one could have looked after me better. I just wish I hadn't been such a nuisance.'

'You weren't. I'm glad I was here. I couldn't bear to think of you being ill and alone.'

He was staring at her again. Lauren looked away. 'I'd have got over it. I'll tell Anna what a good doctor you are and how you looked after a damsel in distress,' she answered, trying to inject some humour into the situation.

They sat chatting for a while. Lauren told Glenn about her childhood and how she had come to know Anna. She felt that she had to keep mentioning her friend. He listened attentively and then talked a little about his childhood growing up in New York. Lauren thought that his life sounded so exciting in comparison to her dull existence in England, but he seemed really interested in what she had to say. She found him very easy to talk to.

Then Glenn said, 'I think the rain has

stopped and I can't hear the wind any more.'

As he spoke, there was a whirring sound from the air conditioning unit. 'The power's come back,' he told her, switching on the light and the television. 'Let's see what the news is.'

Lauren was pleased to feel the cool breeze on her face. It had become unbearably hot and she was worried that she would start feeling ill again.

They sat watching the news for a while, glad to hear that the storm had moved away and was gradually dying down and that only minor damage had been done in the Bahamian Islands.

'I'm so relieved,' Glenn said. 'Things could have been so much worse.'

* * *

Glenn took Lauren's hand and led her down the stairs to go outside to inspect their surroundings. 'It's safer to walk down, I think,' he said, 'just in case the power goes off again. We don't want to get stuck in the lift.' She tried to pull her hand away, but he said, 'You're still weak, Lauren.'

She gave in. Glenn was right. She didn't feel very strong. She felt safe holding on to him.

Outside, there was no major damage, just a few fallen trees and uprooted shrubs. 'This can soon be cleared up,' Glenn said.

Back upstairs once more, Lauren was glad to sit down. 'How's your leg now?' Glenn asked.

'Much better.'

'You don't think you should see a doctor?'

'No. It's fine.'

'And how do you feel?'

'A little weak, but otherwise I'm all right.'

'Good.'

'If you want to go, Glenn, I'll be able to manage on my own now.'

'I'm not going anywhere.'

'But you've got your flight to Washington to sort out.'

'That can wait until I'm sure it's safe to leave you.'

'Look Glenn, it's safe now,' Lauren protested. 'I'm very grateful to you for all you've done, but I've taken up enough of your time.'

'I'll stay around a little longer.'

He came over to her and placed a finger on her lips. 'That's settled,' he said softly.

She looked up into his eyes. Her legs felt weak again and her heart was pounding. This time she knew it wasn't heatstroke that was affecting her. She had to get away from Glenn before she forgot herself and threw her arms around him, so powerful was the effect he had on her.

Glenn stood motionless, gazing at her, his glance never wavering from her eyes. Lauren saw this as if she were watching him in slow motion. She knew what was going to happen but was powerless to stop it.

His arms went round her waist. For a moment he stared into her eyes and then his lips met hers.

Lauren Makes A Decision

'No,' Lauren said, pushing Glenn away. 'We can't do this.' He quickly let go and moved away from her. 'I'm sorry, Lauren. I shouldn't have done that. I didn't mean to upset you.'

'You haven't upset me, but it's all wrong,' she said with a sob. 'You belong to Anna.'

'I'm not so sure about that,' he murmured, 'but I have been going out with her for a few weeks, so I guess I shouldn't kiss her friend, even though she's the most attractive woman I've ever met, and . . . and I think I'm beginning to fall for her.'

'You mustn't say that.' Lauren could feel her cheeks burning.

'I must and I just did.'

'You'd better go, Glenn. You shouldn't say things like that to me. Save them for Anna.'

'I'm only speaking the truth and from your reaction I think that you might have some feelings for me, too. Am I right, Lauren?'

'No,' Lauren said. 'Anna's my friend.' She started to pace up and down.

'And she's mine, too, but that doesn't alter the way I feel.'

'But it should alter the way we act.' Lauren stood and faced him.

'You're right. I shouldn't have kissed you, or presumed that you felt the same way as I did. I'm not being fair to Anna or you. I don't know what came over me. It must be the weather making me act in this way.

'Then, seeing you so ill. I was so worried about you that when you made such a rapid recovery, the relief just went to my head. Can you forgive me? It won't happen again.'

Lauren knew it wouldn't happen again. She'd make sure of that, but it would be so difficult. She wanted to rush into Glenn's arms and stay there forever, but she couldn't do that. They had Anna to consider.

'Can you forgive me?' he repeated.

'There's nothing to forgive. I'm as much to blame as you.'

'Lauren! You . . . you don't mean . . .'

'I don't mean anything,' she said quickly. 'I just think that we should forget any of this happened. For Anna's sake.'

'Yes, yes, of course. Well, I guess I'd better go now, if you're sure you'll be okay.'

'Quite sure, and thanks, Glenn, for looking after me.'

He took hold of her hand, squeezed it and said, 'It was a pleasure.' All traces of his former display of passion had gone. Lauren didn't know whether to feel pleased or disappointed.

* * *

Glenn rang for a cab and was told that it would be there in a few minutes.

Lauren sat down while he collected up his things, trying to stop the tears from running down her cheeks, knowing that this was probably the last time she would ever be on her own with him.

He came into the lounge. 'I'm ready now,' he said. Then, seeing her tear-stained face, he rushed over and took hold of her hands. 'What is it Lauren? Are you feeling ill again?'

'N . . . no,' she sobbed, pulling away. 'Just go. I'll be all right.'

'I can't leave you like this. Please tell me what's wrong.'

'It's better I don't.' She wiped her eyes.

'Why?' He sat down beside her. She could see the look of hope that had sprung into his eyes. 'Why?' he repeated.

Lauren stood up and turned away from him. 'Go, Glenn. Please.'

'But Lauren . . . '

'No, Glenn. Don't say any more.'

'If that's what you really want.' His voice was clipped and harsh. He strode to the door and walked out without looking back.

As soon as he was gone, the tears came again. Why had she come on this holiday? It was meant to be the experience of a lifetime. But she would remember it as a time of misery, when she had fallen desperately in love with someone she couldn't have.

For years, ever since Jake, she'd never let her feelings run away with her. Why had she fallen for Glenn so deeply and so quickly? She'd thought she was immune to such things. She'd never believed in love at first sight. Yet this was what it had been with Glenn. She knew that now.

Lauren clasped and unclasped her hands. How would she be able to act normally in front of Anna when she returned from England? The situation was impossible. She had to go home now, at once. She couldn't stay here any longer. But how could she explain this to Anna? She'd have to think up some excuse. Then Lauren wondered if the flights to England were running normally. After all, there had been a tropical storm and she didn't know what the current weather forecast was. Had there been any damage at the airport that would stop the flights from taking off?

She gradually calmed down. If she could get home, she would leave an excuse with Catherine. Maybe she'd say she was needed back at work urgently.

She'd ask Michael if it was possible for him to meet her, and explain to him that Anna had returned to England to be with her father, and she'd been on her own in Nassau long enough.

Lauren dialled the airport. She got the engaged signal.

Some time later, the telephone rang. It was Catherine, asking how she was getting on. Lauren thought it best not to tell her she'd been ill. After chatting about the weather and the storm for a few minutes, Catherine asked, 'Is Glenn still there?'

'No. He left a little while ago.'

'Oh, I thought he might have stayed a bit longer. You must have been glad of his company. Has he gone to Washington?'

'I don't know. I suppose he will when he can get a flight.'

'I guess he needs to get back to work as soon as possible. Anyway, I'll come over to see you now.'

'No. That's not necessary. Look, Catherine, I . . . I think I'll go home when I can get a flight.'

'What? But why? Anna will probably be back in a couple of days. And I'm sure it won't be long before the weather improves.'

'I know. But I've been here over a week and I've been enough of a burden to everyone.'

'Of course you haven't. I've thoroughly enjoyed myself taking you around, doing all the touristy things I don't normally do. Besides, there are still plenty of places to see. I'm sure Glenn didn't mind looking after you, either.'

Lauren didn't know how to answer that, so she didn't try. She made an effort to sound decisive. 'I'll let you know when I've made my plans. Don't worry about me. I've thoroughly enjoyed myself. Thank you so much for all you and Peter have done. I'll be in touch later. I'd better go now.'

Lauren hung up before Catherine could say anything else. She'd made her decision now and she wouldn't be persuaded to change it. Then a thought crossed her mind. What if Anna rang up, or, worse still, Glenn tried to get in touch with her? She disconnected the phone and switched off her mobile. Then she went into the bedroom, lay on the bed and slept.

Later, when she was rested, she reconnected the phone and got through to the airport. She got a flight out for the next day. The airline staff were very understanding. A lot of people had made changes to their itineraries because of the tropical storm.

She rang Michael. He was relieved to hear that she was all right. 'I've been trying to ring you for ages,' he said. 'I knew the lines were down yesterday, but I thought they would be okay today. I kept getting the unobtainable signal. I was so worried. And your mobile seemed dead, too.'

'All the phones have been affected,' Lauren said. She then had a long discussion with her brother, who tried to persuade her to finish her holiday in Nassau.

'No, I've quite made up my mind,' she told him. 'Anyway, I've changed my flight now, so I'll have to come home.'

Michael agreed to meet Lauren at the airport. He'd take a few hours off work to drive her home, but he couldn't stay, he told her. It was a very busy period.

This suited Lauren. She didn't want to say too much about her visit to Nassau. She wasn't sure if she could talk about it without becoming emotional.

She tried to convince herself that once she was thousands of miles away, back in her normal routine, things wouldn't seem so bad. She disconnected the phone again, packed her suitcase, tidied up Anna's flat and then sank down exhausted on the bed. She still felt very weak and was glad that the air conditioning was working. She didn't even think to glance at her mobile phone.

Lauren slept till morning. She booked a taxi for later in the day, had a last look round the flat, ventured outside briefly, then went inside and reconnected the phone so she could let Catherine know what she was doing.

'Anna's been trying to ring you,' Catherine told her. 'And I couldn't get through either. I thought all the lines were okay again.'

'I suppose there must still be trouble with some lines,' Lauren replied, feeling terrible that she was giving her friends so much bother, but it was for the best. It was better for them that she left.

Catherine wanted to take Lauren to the airport, but she assured her there was no need as a taxi was booked. Once again she thanked her for all she had done and asked her to explain to Anna why she had left. 'But I don't understand why you're going,' Catherine protested.

Lauren just said that she'd taken up enough of their time and would be contacting Anna after she got home.

The flight back to England was unremarkable. Lauren sat next to a young woman who spent most of the time sleeping or reading. She missed the companionship of Sadie, which she'd had on the outward journey. That seemed like a lifetime ago. In such a short while her life had changed so much.

* * *

Michael met Lauren at the airport. 'Now what's the real reason you've come back early?' he demanded.

'I told you. Anna was away in England and it wasn't fair to expect her friends to keep ferrying me around, so as soon as it was safe to travel after the tropical storm, I thought I'd better just come home.'

'But Anna will be back in Nassau soon. You said that her father was getting on well.'

Lauren had known that she'd have a hard time convincing Michael that she'd done the right thing. After all, he was her brother and he knew her so well. 'Yes, he is,' she replied, 'but Anna will have things to do when she gets home. She wouldn't have wanted me tagging along.'

'Don't be silly. She's your best friend. Besides, she invited you to stay. It was to have been a holiday of a lifetime.'

'It was.' He'll never know how much, Lauren thought. 'Look, Michael, I'm home now, so there's no point in saying anything else. It's too late to ponder on whether I've done the right thing.'

'Okay, I'll keep quiet, but I know there's more to this than meets the eye. Still, if you don't want to discuss it, that's fine,' he said, giving Lauren a penetrating look.

I don't like keeping secrets, Lauren thought, but I can't tell him the real reason I didn't stay in Nassau.

Anna, too, was upset by Lauren's decision. She phoned her from her parents' house. 'You shouldn't have left like that, Lauren,' she said. 'I'm going back to Nassau tomorrow. I was really looking forward to seeing you again. There was still so much I wanted to show you. I think Catherine's a bit put out, too. I thought you liked her. She said she was enjoying showing you around.'

'I do like her. She was brilliant, but I couldn't keep taking up her time.'

'What about Glenn? Did he know you were leaving? I gather he went to Washington as soon as he could after the storm. It's a pity he wasn't able to stay longer. Couldn't you get on with him? Was that what it was?' Anna went on. 'Right from when you first arrived, I had a feeling you didn't like him.'

'Of course I got on with him. I'm

sorry if I've offended you, Anna, but at the time I thought I was doing the right thing.' She tried to sound conciliatory. 'Maybe I should have stayed, but it's too late now.'

Anna wanted to call in to see Lauren before she returned to Nassau. Lauren managed to persuade her not to come. 'As I've still got a few days before I have to go back to work, I thought I'd go and see my Great Aunt Hilda,' she said. 'She's not been too well recently. She must be getting on for ninety now. She's moved to a residential home near Swansea.'

'All right, I'll take the hint,' Anna said. 'You don't want to see me. You don't need to go making up stories about great-aunts.'

'No it's not that,' Lauren said desperately. 'I do have a great-aunt, and it seemed like a good idea to see her, as I have a few free days.'

What a mess I've got myself into, Lauren thought. Because I've stupidly fallen in love with my best friend's boyfriend, I'm having to continually tell lies, make up excuses and alienate all the people I care about.

* * *

The rest of the holiday flew past. Lauren enjoyed a few days in Swansea so she could visit her great aunt. She hadn't intended doing this, but after telling Anna that was what she was going to do, she decided she'd better do it.

Lauren had difficulty sleeping. She kept seeing pictures of Glenn in her mind and she couldn't forget what had happened between them. Every moment was etched on her mind.

Her aunt noticed the dark circles under her eyes. 'You look tired dear,' she said.

'I'm all right,' Lauren replied. 'I'm just suffering from jet lag.' That was partly the case, she thought, but not the main reason for her sleeplessness. You've got to get Glenn out of your mind, she told herself. He's back with Anna now. He'll have forgotten you.

But had he? Didn't he say he was falling for her? Had she imagined that? No, but it was only because the two of them were thrust together in close proximity, due to the tropical storm, she reasoned. He didn't mean it. What if he did, though?

The argument went round and round in her mind, but there was no resolution to it. Glenn belonged to Anna and she would never see him again. Not unless she was invited to their wedding, a little voice in her head whispered. She wouldn't go. She couldn't. That would be too difficult, seeing the man she loved marrying her best friend.

Maybe they wouldn't get married. Perhaps they'd split up. Then you'd have a chance. Lauren tried to quell that treacherous voice. It was no use having false hopes. Glenn was lost to her. She had to accept that.

Lauren's work colleagues were eager

to hear about her holiday and wondered how the tropical storm had affected it. She didn't really want to discuss that, but everyone kept talking about it, and wanted to know all the details. She showed them photos of Nassau before the storm and talked about the places she had visited. She made sure that she didn't show them the one photo she had of Glenn, taken on the night she went with him and Anna to the Junkanoo restaurant. He was standing next to Anna, who looked so happy. He had taken one of her and Anna together, too.

* * *

When Lauren returned home from work that night, Michael wasn't there. After she'd had dinner, she took out the photograph of Glenn and Anna and sat and stared at it. His arm was placed protectively around her, and she was smiling contentedly. I should be feeling pleased for her, not consumed by jealousy, Lauren chided herself. Anna deserves to be happy after what Rob did to her.

But don't you also deserve happiness? a little voice in her head whispered. What Jake did to you was no better. He was already engaged to someone else and hadn't bothered to tell you. But that was years ago, she reminded herself. You've been over that for a long time.

What about Glenn, though? What are his feelings in all this? If he was really happy with Anna, why did he kiss her and say that he was falling for her? It was all too much for Lauren. She would put the photo of Glenn away and at the same time put him out of her mind. She knew it wouldn't be easy, but she had to try.

* * *

Lauren soon settled back into her old routine at work. It was a busy period, so she stayed late several evenings and hardly saw Michael. By the time she went to bed she was too exhausted to dwell on her problems. Gradually she resumed her normal social life, going out with friends after work for a drink or to the cinema. Lauren felt pleased with herself for the way she was coping. She tried to act in her old cheerful manner and was sure that no-one would guess that inside her heart was breaking.

Anna sent Lauren several emails giving details of her father's progress and of her return to Nassau. She told her that Catherine had enjoyed her company and was sorry that Lauren had left so abruptly. She also mentioned that Glenn was still away in Washington and that she hadn't seen him yet, but they kept in touch as often as possible.

Michael, too, was very busy. Lauren had seen little of her brother since her return from the Bahamas. He always left before her in the morning and came home very late. He hadn't asked her again what the real reason was for cutting short her holiday. He'd seemed rather pre-occupied and only glanced briefly at her photographs. Lauren was beginning to get worried about him. He was working too hard, she thought.

'I never see you,' she said one evening as he returned home just before midnight. 'It's not right, you having to work such long hours.'

Michael looked a bit sheepish, Lauren thought. He sat down beside her on her sofa and took her hand.

'Er . . . Lauren, I haven't actually been working all the time. I was meaning to tell you . . . '

'What is it Michael? Are you all right? You're not ill, are you?'

'No, of course not. It's just that I've . . . '

'You've what Michael? Tell me.'

'It's just that I've . . . I've met someone,' he blurted out.

Lauren sighed with relief. 'I was getting worried in case there was something wrong.'

'You always worry about everything, but don't confide in anyone when you have a problem,' he chided.

'That's not true.'

'It is. And I know there's more to it as to why you left the Bahamas in such a hurry.'

'We're not talking about me,' Lauren said quickly, 'we're discussing you. Now tell me, who have you met? I want to hear all about her.'

'She's called Joanna, Jo for short. And we're . . . we're thinking of moving in together. What do you say Lauren? Would you mind?'

'Well, it is a bit of a shock, but I'm glad you've met someone, and of course it's up to you what you do.'

It was true, she was pleased for her brother, but at this particular period of time, it only seemed to emphasise her own unhappiness. Lauren felt her eyes prick with tears. She blinked them away before Michael could see them. She'd always known that one day he would leave the flat and she would be on her own, but she hadn't banked on it happening just now, when she felt so alone.

'Where did you meet Jo? How long have you known her? When can I meet her? Why haven't you mentioned her before?'

'Hold on a minute,' Michael laughed. 'One question at a time. I met her at a works do a few months ago. She's in the same firm as me but in a different department.'

'So when I thought you were working all hours, you were going out with Jo?'

'Well, yes, but some of the time I was doing overtime. We have been very busy. I didn't mention her before because I didn't know how things were going to work out. I thought it might all come to nothing. I haven't been very successful in my love life so far.'

'Are you referring to Anna?'

'What makes you say that?'

'I had a feeling you had a thing about her.'

'Well, I must admit that I was pretty

keen on her when we were younger. I did waste rather a lot of time hoping that something would happen between us, but it never did. I think she only saw me as a brother.'

'I had hoped you and Anna would get together, too,' Lauren confessed. 'But you think you'll stay with Jo?'

'I want to marry her, Lauren.'

'Oh, it's all so exciting,' Lauren exclaimed, glad to share her brother's happiness.

'But, what about you, Lauren? Is there anybody special for you?'

'No,' she answered briefly. 'Now, when can I meet Jo?'

'Very soon, I hope. We'll have to arrange something. But do you think you can manage living on your own, Lauren?'

'Of course. I'm not a child.'

'I know that. But after Mum died, I said I would always take care of you.'

'And you have. But you can't spend all your time with me. You've got to make your own life.'

'And so have you. I wish you could find someone, Lauren.'

'Don't worry about me.'

'You're not still pining for Jake, are you? It was so long ago. You've got to move on.'

'No, Michael, I got over Jake years ago. Look, you go ahead and be with Jo. I'm happy on my own.' That was partly true. She had been happy until she'd met Glenn and she would be again when she succeeded in getting him out of her system. 'What does Jo look like?' she asked.

'Gorgeous, but then I'm prejudiced. I just wish Mum could have known her.'

'I still miss Mum so much. It all seems so unfair. She wasn't old. She was always helping everyone, but in the end no-one could help her.' Lauren couldn't stop a tear from escaping.

Michael quickly put his arm around her. 'I know how you feel, sis, but it's no use dwelling on it. She's gone and there's nothing we can do about it, except carry on as best we can. That's what she would have wanted.'

'You're right.' Lauren wiped her eyes and asked, 'Where will you live?'

'We're thinking of renting a flat while we try and arrange a mortgage. Somewhere not too far away, so I'll be able to keep an eye on you.'

'That won't be necessary. I'm sure I'll manage quite well,' Lauren said. 'But I admit it will be nice to know you're not too far away.'

* * *

Lauren couldn't sleep. Thoughts of Michael, Jo, Anna and Glenn chased round and round in her head. Now she knew why, for all these years, her brother had not had a serious girlfriend. He'd always been interested in Anna, but she hadn't reciprocated. He must have been heartbroken when Anna got involved with Rob, but I never suspected anything, Lauren mused. He didn't say a word. Now he's got over her and found someone else, so there's hope for you, she told herself. But that little voice in her head whispered, no, it is too late for you. No-one will ever compare to Glenn.

Lauren wondered how she would get on with living on her own. Although she'd assured Michael that she'd be all right, she was a little nervous about it, because it would be a new experience for her. But she was grown up now. It would soon be her twenty-fifth birthday. She'd cope, she resolved.

* * *

Two days later Michael was packing up his possessions. Lauren helped him load up his car and then travelled with him to his new flat, which wasn't too far away.

'You can come round for coffee one evening,' he promised, 'and meet Jo.'

Lauren had coffee with Michael and Jo a few days later. She was greeted with great warmth and enthusiasm. 'I'm so pleased to meet you. I've heard such a lot about you,' Jo said. 'I've always wished I had a sister. I'm sure we're going to get on just fine.'

Lauren thought so, too.

When Michael rang up the next evening to see how Lauren was, he told her that Jo really liked her and was hoping she'd come round again soon. 'So what did you think of her?' he asked.

'She's lovely and so pretty. You've made a very good choice. I couldn't have picked anyone better for you myself!'

'And how are you coping alone?'

'Fine, thanks.'

That was true. She felt as if she were beginning to get her life back together again. She was seeing friends and was feeling more cheerful than she had for a long time. Of course, she missed her brother, but she was genuinely glad that he was so happy.

Then a few days later, soon after Lauren arrived home from work, her phone rang. She picked up the receiver. 'Hello?'

'Hi, Lauren. It's Glenn.'

Glenn Declares His Feelings

There could be no mistaking that deep, American drawl. 'W . . . what do you want?' Laura stammered. 'is something wrong with Anna?' Why else would he be ringing? Her heart was beating madly. She didn't want this. Not now when she was trying so hard to forget him. She sat down, clasping the receiver tightly

'Nothing's wrong with Anna. I wanted to speak to you.

'How are you? Have you recovered from the heatstroke?'

'That was ages ago, I'm quite well now, thank you. Why do you want to speak to me?'

'I think we need to talk, Lauren.'

'No, we don't. There's nothing to talk about.'

'But I think there is. Can I come round?'

'Come round? But where are you?'

'I left Washington yesterday. I'm in England. Can I come round?' he repeated.

'How did you know my telephone number?'

'Anna told me?'

'You asked Anna?'

'Yes.'

'But why? What excuse did you give for asking?'

'Actually, she thought it would be a good idea if I came round to see you.'

'She what?'

'Lauren, this isn't getting us very far.' She could hear the note of exasperation which had crept into his voice. 'Can I come round?'

'No. I don't think that's a good idea.'

'But it is. Look Lauren, Anna's worried about you. She said that if I was in England, perhaps I could look you up. She doesn't understand why you left Nassau in such a hurry. She guesses it must have been the storm which frightened you away, but I don't think it was.'

'Just tell her that I'm OK. And I am rather busy at the moment. I'll have to go. Bye Glenn.'

She hung up.

She was trembling all over, and her eyes were pricking with tears. If only he hadn't rung, she thought. He's brought back so many memories I wanted to forget. She sat staring at the phone and jumped when it rang again. I won't answer it, she decided. But it kept on ringing. Supposing it's not Glenn and it's something important, she mused. Finally she gave in and picked up the receiver.

'I knew you'd answer in the end,' Glenn said. 'I wasn't going to give up, you know.'

'I thought it might be something important. That's why I answered.

'I didn't know it was you ringing back.'

'Thanks Lauren, you make a guy feel so wanted!'

'Glenn, I don't think there's anything else to say.'

'But there is. Please Lauren, let me come round. I do need to talk to you.'

She wanted to refuse. She knew that was what she should have done, but the thought of seeing him again was so tempting.

'Are you still there?' Glenn said.

'Yes. I was thinking.'

'What about? Were you going to say yes?'

'I'm not sure,' she replied hesitantly. Maybe, as Anna had suggested he should come round, he'd better do it, Lauren thought, otherwise, her friend might wonder why.

'As I said before,' Glenn went on, 'Anna thinks the storm frightened you away, but it wasn't that, was it? It was because of what happened between us. That's it, isn't it?'

Lauren sighed. She couldn't fight it any longer. 'You know that's the reason. But I couldn't tell Anna that, so I had to make up something else. Although what I said was partly true. I was a burden to everyone.'

'Not to me, Lauren. You could never be that. So, have you decided? Can I come round?'

'I don't know.'

'We really do need to talk, and I wanted to say I was sorry for ruining your holiday.'

'There's nothing to talk about and you didn't ruin my holiday. I don't know why you think that. You kissed me once. That was a mistake. Now we've both got to forget about it.'

'I can't. And was that all it was to you? Just a mistake?'

'What else could it be? Anna's my friend. If she knew about us, she'd be heartbroken.'

'I'm not so sure about that.'

Her heart was racing so fast, it felt as if it would burst. 'Of course she would,' Lauren stated firmly, but at the same time a little voice in the back of her mind was asking, why is he saying that?

'Look, let me come round for half an

hour. Then I promise to go.

'Anna will wonder why I didn't come to see you.'

That was true, Lauren thought. Anna will think that the reason I wouldn't see Glenn was because I didn't like him. She'd already asked if that was the case. Lauren hesitated. 'When did you want to come?'

'Tomorrow evening, if possible. I have to return to Nassau the day after.'

'All right. Come at eight o'clock. I'll have coffee ready. Do you know where to come?'

'Yes, of course. I've looked it up.'

'Oh. OK, I'll see you then.'

'I'm looking forward to it. Bye Lauren.'

* * *

She was shaking when she hung up. She slumped onto the settee, trying to calm down. What had she done? She'd resigned herself to never seeing Glenn again, and now he was going to turn up on her own doorstep. Why had she agreed? What good would it do? She had let him persuade her too easily. And why did he seem so unsure of Anna's feelings? Lauren had thought Anna was crazy about Glenn. Could it be that she was still pining over Rob? No. She'd said she wouldn't ever forgive him. Perhaps Anna was too reserved with Glenn and hadn't let him know how she felt. He'd complained once that she was so English.

Whatever it was, Lauren wondered how she was going to cope the next evening, seeing Glenn again and discussing Anna with him, when what she'd really want to do would be to throw her arms around him, and tell him that she loved him. And what about Glenn's feelings? Did he love Anna? If he did, why had he said he was falling for Lauren? She was back to that again.

* * *

Lauren found it hard to concentrate at work the next day. She made several mistakes and had to apologise to her boss, Brian.

'Don't worry about it. You're not usually like this,' he said. 'It's probably the hot weather. I think we're all finding it hard going.'

That was true. They were having unusually warm and humid weather. But Lauren knew that wasn't the reason.

* * *

At eight o'clock precisely the doorbell rang. Lauren made herself walk calmly to the door. She opened it, her heart missing a beat as she saw Glenn looking very rugged in his open necked shirt and chinos.

'Hi Lauren. I hope you don't mind this gear,' he said, as his eyes met hers, 'but it's so hot I had to change after I'd finished work. I think these high temperatures are preparing me for Nassau again.'

She was aware that he was looking at her T-shirt and short skirt. She wondered why she'd put those on? A loose top and longer skirt would have been better. 'It is hot,' she agreed. 'Come and sit down. What would you like to drink? I've got some beer if it's too hot for coffee.'

'Beer'll be fine.'

Glenn sat down on the sofa as Lauren went to the kitchen. She closed the door and tried to catch her breath. What are we going to say to each other, she thought? She remembered that they didn't have any trouble finding things to talk about the night of the storm. But that was before he kissed me and everything changed, she reminded herself. Oh, I feel like a schoolgirl on her first date. But this isn't a date, she chided herself. Glenn's here to talk about Anna. Maybe he wants your advice, as you're her best friend. What can I say, though? All I know is that the man I love is sitting on my sofa, and I've got to tell him how to win the heart of someone else.

Lauren poured out a glass of fruit juice for herself. She really needed something stronger, but didn't dare because of the effect it might have on her. She placed a glass of beer on a tray alongside a plate of biscuits. She took a deep breath, opened the kitchen door and carefully carried in the tray and put it on the coffee table.

She sat down opposite Glenn. Although she tried hard not to, she found her eyes drawn to his. 'Did you have any trouble finding my flat?' she asked.

'No. I found it easily. Got the Tube, then I walked.'

'Don't you hire a car when you're in England?'

'There's no point. I can take the Tube when I'm in London. Much less hassle.'

'Is your father here with you?'

'No, he's back home in the States. I'm the one who has to do the travelling now. As I said before, he's always on the lookout for new hotels and he gets me to sort everything out and check up on our existing hotels at the same time. But Lauren, I didn't come here to talk about my job.'

'What did you come here for?'

'I can't get what happened between us out of my mind.'

'Nothing happened, Glenn.'

'So that kiss was nothing to you? Is that what you're saying? Tell me the truth. It didn't mean anything to you?'

Lauren couldn't lie, but telling the truth was no use, either. 'I'm not saying that,' she murmured.

'What are you saying? Tell me, please.' His eyes never left hers.

'We shouldn't have done it,' was all she could say.

'But we did.'

'Yes, and Anna's your girlfriend, and my best friend. You shouldn't have been kissing me.'

'Since that night I've thought of nothing else.'

'We said we were going to forget

about what happened,' Lauren reminded him.

'I know, but I can't.'

'Anna's my friend. She trusts me. I don't want to hurt her.'

'And the last thing I want to do is hurt Anna, but I can't stop thinking about you.'

'Well you must,' Lauren said firmly.

'Maybe, but it's how I feel. That night when I took you in my arms it felt so right . . . as if you belonged there.'

That was exactly what she'd felt, but she couldn't tell Glenn that.

'The whole time I was in Washington I was thinking about you, wondering if you were okay, wanting to get in touch, but not daring,' he went on.

'So why did you?'

'When I spoke to Anna, she said that I should call round and see how you were.'

'Well, you've seen me, so you can tell her I'm all right. You've done your duty. You can go now.'

Was she really saying this? It was

obvious that Glenn was as attracted to her as she was to him, yet she was dismissing her feelings, pretending they didn't exist. She had to do this for Anna's sake, she kept reminding herself.

'I don't want to go. That's the trouble. And don't talk about duty. I didn't come here out of a sense of duty. I came because I wanted to. I couldn't wait to see you again.'

'Glenn . . . '

'I'm trying to tell you how I feel, Lauren.'

She looked into his eyes. 'Don't say any more, please Glenn,' she whispered.

'I've got to. I can't keep my feelings bottled up any longer. You've put a spell on me, Lauren. I can't get you out of my mind.'

And that was what he had done to her.

He reached for her hand. 'No.' She snatched her hand away. 'You . . . you shouldn't say that. It wasn't real. It was the storm . . . the way we were thrust together, you having to look after me when I was ill . . . '

'Lauren . . . '

'Let me finish. When you get back to Nassau and see Anna again, you'll forget about me. You have to.'

How could she say this when she knew she would never forget him?

She stared at the floor, not daring to face him.

'So you're telling me that I mean nothing to you? Look at me, Lauren. Is that what you're saying? If that's the truth, I'll leave you alone. I won't bother you again.' He came across and knelt down on the floor in front of her.

She lifted her head and gazed straight into those penetrating blue eyes. 'I . . . I . . . ' How could she lie to him? Yet if she revealed the truth, she'd betray her friend.

'Go on,' he urged, gently clasping her hand. 'Do you have any feelings for me?'

This time she didn't resist. How could she, when he was so close she could almost hear his heart beating?

'It's not right, Glenn,' she murmured.

'You mean you do have feelings for me?'

'Yes,' she whispered.

He put his arms around her, pulling her up from the armchair, gazing incredulously into her eyes. 'You've said it at last. I knew I wasn't wrong.'

Lauren looked up at him, wishing things could be different. 'But Glenn, you're Anna's boyfriend. We can't do this to her. Don't you care anything for her?'

'Of course I do. I'm very fond of her, but that's nothing to what I feel for you.'

'Oh, Glenn, this is such a muddle.'

'But we can sort it out.'

Glenn held her closer. Suddenly his lips were on hers. Lauren didn't stop him. She couldn't. This was what she had dreamed of for so long.

* * *

Lauren moved across the room and sat facing him, full of guilt and remorse. 'We shouldn't have done that, Glenn.'

'Probably not. But I wanted it and I believe you did, too. Isn't that true?'

'Yes,' she replied in a small voice, 'but just because we wanted it, doesn't make it right.'

'No, but it's happened and it's confirmed something I've known for a while.'

'What's that?'

'Anna's not the woman for me.'

'She loves you, Glenn,' Lauren said.

'I'm not so sure about that. But even if she does, I'm not the man for her.'

'What makes you doubt her, Glenn?'

'Well, to start with, kissing her is not the same as kissing you. I thought it was just because she was rather shy, in a reserved, English sort of way, but now I suspect that her heart wasn't really in it. So maybe she doesn't care about me.'

Lauren could feel her face burning. Why had she been so abandoned in the way she'd kissed Glenn? She hadn't behaved like this with anyone else. But you've never felt this way before, not even for Jake, a little voice in her head reminded her.

'Oh, Glenn. What if Anna really does love you?'

'I don't think she does.'

'I know you keep saying that, but if she knew I'd come between you, she'd never forgive me. We've been friends for years, since we were children, more like sisters, really, and I don't want to lose that.'

'You haven't done anything wrong, Lauren.'

'She was so unhappy after her engagement to Rob ended,' Lauren went on, as if she hadn't heard what Glenn had said.

'She wouldn't talk about that,' Glenn said. 'What really happened?'

'Oh.' Lauren put her hand to her mouth. 'Perhaps I shouldn't have mentioned Rob.'

'She did tell me she'd been engaged and it hadn't worked out. She'd said that it was all in the past and finished, so I didn't bring it up again, but I guess I should have. It might have helped me to understand her a little better. Is there more I should know?'

'I won't go into details, but Rob hurt her very badly. That was why she left England to make a fresh start. Being offered a teaching post in the Bahamas seemed like an ideal opportunity. I hoped it would help her to get over what happened, and it seemed to have worked. I kept in touch with her regularly and gradually she began to sound much happier. Then, when we were arranging my trip to Nassau, she sent me an email saying there was someone she wanted me to meet, so I guessed she had found another boyfriend. I was glad that things had worked out for her.' Lauren sighed, 'And I don't want to be the cause of any more grief for her.'

'You're not. It's me,' Glenn said. 'Maybe I gave her the wrong impression, although I didn't mean to. I never told her I loved her and she certainly didn't say that to me.'

Lauren stared at him. Perhaps she was the one who had got everything wrong. If Anna wasn't in love with him . . .

'We enjoyed each other's company when I was in Nassau,' Glenn went on, 'but we hadn't really thought about making our relationship permanent in any way. I was content with things as they were. That is, until you came along, Lauren.'

He stood up, moved across the room and sat down in front of her again.

He took hold of her hands and said, 'Lauren, you've bewitched me. I can't get you out of my mind.'

'Glenn, I . . . '

'Let me finish.' He put his finger to her lips. 'I know I've got to sort out my relationship with Anna, but when I've done that, is there . . . is there any hope that we could be together? Please say there is. You did say that you had feelings for me, and . . . and . . . '

'Yes Glenn,' she breathed, 'oh yes, but you've got to see Anna and sort things out properly first. I can't bear hurting her.'

In answer, Glenn pulled Lauren to him and kissed her. She clung to him as if she couldn't bear to let him go.

'I've wanted to do that since the moment I first set eyes on you at the airport,' he murmured. 'Ever since you trod on my foot and looked at me with those enormous green eyes of yours.'

Lauren laughed. 'I was so overcome, I didn't know what to say to you. And I couldn't believe it when I discovered we were on the same flight.'

'Neither could I. And then you had to go and trip over my bag and bump your head.'

'I felt so stupid.'

'And I felt guilty for making you fall over my bag. Yet even then, I had this feeling that somehow we were destined to be together.'

'I hoped so, too, until I discovered you were Anna's new boyfriend. That shattered any dreams I might have had. I resolved that I would put you out of my mind for ever.'

'You mean that you felt something for me even then?'

'Oh, yes. I was bewitched too.'

'I can't believe this is happening,' Glenn exclaimed.

'Neither can I,' Lauren breathed, as their lips met once again.

Several minutes later they pulled away from each other. Glenn said, 'Look Lauren, nice as this is, we've got to stop now and decide what to do.'

'Yes, of course.'

'I'm flying back to Nassau tomorrow. I need to make plans.'

Lauren's heart sank. He was leaving so soon. Her eyes pricked with tears. 'Let Anna down gently,' she urged. 'I don't want her hurt more than she has to be.'

'I'll do my best. Hurting her is the last thing I want to do. I guess I'll probably take my cue from what she says, and then lead up to telling her that

I think it's best if we finish.'

'What if she asks if there's anyone else?'

'I can't lie.'

'No, but don't say it's me. Not yet. Please, Glenn.'

'Okay, but she'll have to know in the end.'

'Yes, but let me think this out and work out the best way to tell her.'

'Anything you say, Lauren.' He pulled her into his arms again. 'I'll have to go now.'

A tear ran down Lauren's cheek and Glenn kissed it away. 'It's not for ever. We have the rest of our lives ahead of us. And I'll be back in England as soon as I can.'

'I know. But I'll miss you.'

'And I'll miss you too,' he breathed. 'Please don't cry.' He gently wiped her eyes, smiled and said, 'I still can't get my head round all this. A few hours ago, I didn't know whether you even cared a little for me, yet now we're saying we can't bear to be apart.'

Lauren blinked back another tear as she said, 'We mustn't forget Anna. If it wasn't for her, I'd be the happiest girl in the world. But I don't want to be happy at her expense.'

'I'm sure I'll be able to sort things out.'

'I hope so.'

They clung together until Lauren pulled away saying, 'That's my phone. I'll have to answer it. It might be important.'

'Okay.'

Lauren picked up the phone, then sat down, took a deep breath, and as brightly as she could, said, 'Hello, Anna.'

'How are you Lauren? I just thought I would see if everything's all right.'

'Everything's fine. Why shouldn't it be?' She tried to sound as cheerful as possible. 'More to the point, how are you? And how is your father now?'

'I'm very well and my dad is a lot better, thanks.'

'That's good.'

'Glenn will be arriving back in Nassau soon,' Anna went on. 'I can't wait to see him. I've missed him so much. Did he visit you by the way? I suggested that he did.'

'Yes. Actually, Anna, he's still here. He was just about to leave when you rang.' She felt she had to tell Anna this.

'Oh, would you mind if I had a word with him? I'm glad he came to see you. There's such a lot I want to tell him.'

'Anna, I'll . . . ' Lauren tried to interrupt.

'I guess I've always been a bit nervous with Glenn,' Anna continued, ignoring Lauren. 'I think it's because he's so good-looking. I probably haven't treated him too well, either, so I feel I've got to make it up to him somehow. You see, I was so upset by what Rob did that I wouldn't let . . . '

'I'll get him for you,' Lauren interrupted forcefully. She didn't want to hear this.

She beckoned to Glenn.

* * *

Lauren hurried into the kitchen. She couldn't listen to Glenn talking to Anna. She switched the kettle on, sat down at the breakfast bar and put her head in her hands. Now what were they going to do? Only a short time before she had begun to believe that Glenn was right and that Anna wasn't in love with him, but now those ideas were shattered. Anna obviously did love him and wanted to make sure he knew.

The sound of the water bubbling in the kettle roused her. Lauren got up and made herself a strong cup of coffee.

As she sipped the hot drink, the words, *Glenn loves you, not Anna,* kept echoing round and round in her head. That was what he'd implied, hadn't he? Surely she hadn't imagined it. Oh, whatever they did, Anna was going to get hurt. Unless . . .

'I could do with a coffee myself,' Glenn said.

'I didn't hear you come in,' she

responded, quickly getting up. 'I'll make you one if you have time. But I thought you had to go,' she added.

'I did, but everything's changed.' He turned her to face him, kissing her tear-stained face. 'We've got to alter our plans, Lauren.'

'I know,' she murmured, pouring out his coffee. 'Let's go and sit down.' She knew what he was going to say and she didn't want to hear it. Just for a few moments she had believed that her wildest dream might come true, but in an instant all her hopes had been dashed.

'You're going back to Anna, aren't you?' she said in a small voice, when they were seated side by side on the sofa.

Glenn put his coffee down and pulled Lauren close to him. 'I'm not saying that.'

'But what else can you do? She loves you.'

'And I love you, Lauren.'

He'd said it, she thought, but it

didn't make her feel any happier. She couldn't wreck Anna's life. She'd have to be strong and send him away.

'Did you hear me? I love you,' Glenn repeated. 'And I think you love me too. Is that correct? Please answer, Lauren.'

'I . . . I . . . ' What could she say?

'Do you love me?'

'Yes.' She couldn't deny it. 'But . . . '

'No buts.'

'Listen, Glenn,' Lauren said firmly. 'You met Anna first. We can't ruin her life just because we've been stupid enough to fall for each other. She comes first. If she found out about us she'd go to pieces. She did after she found out about Rob. I didn't think she'd ever get over that. She was completely devastated. And to have the same thing happen to her again would be more than she could bear.'

'Anna's probably a lot tougher than you think. After her broken engagement, she picked herself up and travelled to the other side of the world. That's not the action of someone weak.

Could you have done that?'

Lauren didn't want to answer. When Jake had left she'd stayed at home, trying to rebuild her life there, with the help of her mother and her brother.

'But I'm her best friend,' Lauren said. 'How can I be the one who causes her so much pain?'

'I know it's going to be difficult, but I've got to finish with her, Lauren. I can't stay with Anna when it's you I love. It wouldn't be fair to her.'

'Oh, Glenn, what are we going to do?' She leaned against him and he put his arms around her.

'I'll find a way. I'll go back tomorrow as planned. Then, when I see her, I'll have to gradually lead up to telling her.'

'Don't let her know about me. Not yet. Please, Glenn.'

'Okay.'

'I'd like to tell her myself.'

'I can understand that. Now, I really have got to go.' He gave Lauren one last lingering kiss. 'I'll be in touch when I've spoken to Anna,' he promised, 'but it won't be for a few days. As well as sorting things out with Anna, I need to do some work and I'll be doing a fair bit of travelling, too. Besides, I think we both need a cooling-off period, don't you?'

She knew he was right, but at the same time dreaded seeing him walk away. It would be a long time before they'd meet again and who knew what might happen when he was back in the Bahamas?

'Don't worry, Lauren, everything will be all right. Trust me,' he said, hugging her close.

Reluctantly she disentangled herself from his embrace, opened the door and stood watching as he walked away.

Lauren Hears About Glenn And Anna

Lauren tried very hard to get back into her normal routine, but she found it difficult. She couldn't stop thinking about what had happened between her and Glenn. He'd promised that everything would be all right, but she wasn't so sure, and as each day went past, and she didn't hear from him, her doubts began to surface.

Saturday came and she still hadn't heard from Glenn. She was beside herself with worry. What was happening? Had he told Anna? He'd said he would be in touch when he had something to report, so obviously there was nothing to tell, she reasoned. But supposing Anna had taken it so badly he'd decided to stay with her? What would she do then? These thoughts were whirling round and round in her head.

On Sunday she awoke late, having only got off to sleep at four o'clock. It's a good thing I don't have to go to work, she yawned. She crawled out of bed and was putting on her dressing gown, when she noticed a red light flashing on her answer phone. Someone called during the night, she thought, or maybe early this morning, and I didn't hear it. Then it dawned on her, it must have been Glenn. And I missed his call! What did he have to say? Her heart started to beat faster. She quickly pressed the button on the answer phone. She suppressed a feeling of disappointment when she heard a female voice. It was Anna.

'I'll probably be arriving on Tuesday,' Lauren heard Anna saying. The line wasn't good and it was difficult to understand her. Lauren pressed the button again and strained to hear. It sounded as if Anna's father had been taken ill again and she was flying back to England. She ended the call, saying, 'I need to see you.'

Lauren debated with herself when to ring Anna. I can't do it yet, as it will only be five o'clock in Nassau, she thought. But if I leave it until much later, she might not be there. Maybe if I wait, and ring at about one, that'll be a good time to catch her, before she goes out. Do I want to hear what she has to say though?

I think she's coming to England because her father has had a relapse, but why does she especially want to see me? Has Glenn told her about us? Is that why? But he promised he wouldn't. I don't think he would break a promise. Has Anna guessed? But why should she? She doesn't know what went on when we were together. I suppose she just wants someone to talk to about her father. Maybe that's why she needs to see me, Lauren concluded.

The time seemed to pass very slowly. Every few minutes Lauren glanced at her watch to see if it was time to ring Anna.

At last, at one o'clock, she picked up the phone and dialled Anna's number. There was no reply at first and Lauren was just going to hang up when her friend answered breathlessly, 'Hello?'

'Anna. It's Lauren here. How are you? How's your Dad? I'm sorry I missed your call. I haven't got you out of bed, have I?'

'Lauren, thank you for ringing back. Actually, I was still in bed.'

'Oh, sorry.'

'That's all right. I had a late night and didn't sleep very well, but it's time I was up. There's a lot to do.'

'So how is everything?' Lauren asked, her heart thumping.

'Not good, I'm afraid.'

'In what way?'

'Well, as I said before, my dad is very bad.'

'I'm sorry Anna, but the telephone line was so bad, I couldn't make out what you were saying. I guessed it was about your dad, and that he'd had a relapse.'

'That's right. He needs another operation. It's really serious this time, worse than before. My mum's in a terrible state. I said I'd come and stay with her. I'm flying home tonight.'

'I am sorry, Anna.'

'It's a good thing it's still the school holiday, but I don't know if I'll be back in time for the new term to begin. I'll have to see how everything goes. My mum keeps panicking about what she'll do if Dad doesn't get better. She's worked herself up into such a state.'

'They'll keep your job open for you, won't they?' Lauren asked.

'I hope so. I'm on a permanent contract, so they should, but I won't stay away longer than I have to.'

'No. You've really enjoyed it in Nassau, haven't you?'

'Yes. It took a while to get used to being away from my parents and England, but now I'm so glad I went there, especially since . . . well, since meeting Glenn. It's the best thing that's ever happened to me.'

'How is he?' Lauren asked, trying to sound casual, her heart in her mouth. 'Have you . . . seen him since he returned?'

'Not yet, but he's coming round later to take me to the airport. We've had so little time together, recently. I've missed him so much, but I don't know if he's missed me. I'd like to think he has, though.'

Lauren thought it was a good thing Anna couldn't see her face. She could feel it burning with guilt. She was also thinking that if Anna hadn't seen Glenn yet, then he hadn't told her that he wanted to finish with her. Lauren knew he wouldn't do that when he was driving Anna to the airport. Maybe he would never tell her. He wouldn't want to hurt her, and she was suffering enough at the moment, worrying about her father and how her mother was coping.

'Are you still there?' Lauren heard Anna saying.

'Yes sorry, the line's bad again,' Lauren lied.

'Anyway, what I wanted to ask you was, would you be able to come and visit me when I'm in England? It would be so nice to see you again. I want to ask your advice about Glenn.'

'I'm no good at advising anyone,' Lauren answered quickly. 'Look at the mess I made of my relationship with Jake, and I haven't exactly had much success since then!'

'That was years ago,' Anna said. 'You weren't much more than a child then.'

'But old enough to think that Jake was going to marry me . . . until I found out that he already had a fiancée.'

'It wasn't your fault that it all went wrong.'

'No, but it doesn't qualify me to give advice to anyone else.'

'Look, I'll have to go now,' Anna said. 'I'll be in touch as soon as I can. Is that all right?'

'Of course it is.'

'Bye Lauren. See you soon.'

'Bye Anna, and I hope the news about your dad will be better when you see him.'

* * *

Lauren put the phone down, feeling more depressed than ever. She was full of remorse about betraying her friend, but at the same time, full of misery for herself, not knowing when, or if, she would ever see Glenn again. And if she did see him, how could she hurt Anna? It was obvious she was in love with him.

Lauren decided she would have to forget about him. That's all she could do. We'll have to try and forget our feelings.

We'll get over it, she tried to reassure herself.

But she didn't believe it.

A few minutes after she'd hung up, almost as if by telepathy, Glenn rang.

'Hello, Lauren. I'm sorry I haven't

been in touch before, but I've been so busy. How are you doing?'

'I'm okay, thanks. What about you?'

'I'm fine. Just rather tired. Look, Lauren, I know you must be wondering, but I haven't told Anna anything yet. I'm taking her to the airport soon. Her father's very ill again, so she's got to go back to the UK.'

'I know. I've just spoken to her.'

'What did she say? How's her father?'

'He's very bad. She . . . she said that she's missed you. Oh Glenn, we can't do anything to hurt her.'

'I don't want to, but I don't see how we can avoid it.'

'We've got to be strong. We shouldn't even be talking now. Anna needs you, Glenn.'

'And you don't?'

'I didn't say that.'

'What are you saying, Lauren?'

'I don't know, Glenn.'

'This line's not very clear. I'll have to go now, but I think we should do some talking. We can't do it over the phone.

I'll be in London again in a few days. I'll come and see you then.'

'But Anna will be here.'

'She doesn't have to know.'

'But going behind her back is . . . is deceitful.'

'Look, Lauren, we've got to sort this out.'

'Have we?'

'Yes, we have. What's the matter with you? You seem to have changed.'

'No, I haven't changed, but the circumstances have. It was all a dream, Glenn. We got carried away by . . . by . . . the storm.'

'It was more than that, and you know it was. But Lauren, I really do have to go. Bye. I love you.'

And before she could say anything else, he'd hung up.

Lauren sat down and cried bitter tears of despair. Glenn didn't seem to realise how difficult the situation was.

He thought that everything could be solved with a little discussion, but

Lauren knew that was not possible. Anna was her best friend and she didn't intend hurting her, whatever Glenn might say.

She'd have to find a way of convincing him that he should stay with Anna, even though doing so would break her heart.

Sometimes you had to sacrifice your own happiness for the sake of someone else, and this was one of those times.

* * *

Two days later, Lauren came home from work and found a message on her answerphone from Anna, informing her that she was now in England and had been to the hospital. Her father had had the operation and was in a stable, but still serious, condition. She ended the message by saying, 'Will you be able to come over and see me?'

Lauren rang back at once. 'Would you like me to come to the hospital with you?' she asked.

'No, only the family are allowed in, but if you could come over on Saturday evening and stay the night, we could have a good chat, like old times. What do you say Lauren?'

Lauren hesitated for just a moment. She really did want to see Anna and anyway, how could she refuse without it sounding odd?

'If you're sure your mum won't mind,' she said.

'No, she'll be delighted. She says it's so long since she's seen you.'

'How is she now?'

'Much better now Dad's operation's over, more positive. The doctors seem hopeful too, so we'll just have to keep our fingers crossed.'

Lauren was pleased that Anna sounded so cheerful, but she was dreading seeing her. She's going to tell me all the gory details about her feelings for Glenn, and I don't want to hear them, but I can't refuse to listen. Oh, why is life so complicated? Other people just meet someone, fall in love and get married. Why do I have to be different and fall for my best friend's man?

* * *

When Saturday arrived, Lauren woke with a splitting headache. I'll be glad when Monday comes, she thought. I just want to get the next two days over with. What is Anna going to say about Glenn? And how am I supposed to react when she pours out her heart to me?

She slept on the train journey and nearly missed getting off at the right station. She grabbed her overnight bag and dived out of the door just before it closed. She'd felt out of sorts all day, and was even worse now. It's all this stress, she told herself. Why do I have to put myself through all of this? I could have refused to come. Anna's your best friend, she chided, she needs you. But what about my feelings? Aren't they important too? Forget yourself, and concentrate on Anna. That's what you must do.

* * *

Lauren arrived at Anna's just after they had returned from the hospital. 'We've only been home ten minutes,' Anna informed her, giving Lauren a big hug. 'I'm so glad you've come. It was better news today. The doctor is very pleased with Dad's progress.'

'That's good news,' Lauren replied.

'He'll have to stay in Intensive Care a bit longer yet, and then he'll be transferred to the High Dependency Unit for a few days before going on to the normal ward, if everything continues to go well.'

* * *

Anna, her mother and Lauren sat drinking coffee and chatting about old times.

'I think I'll have an early night,'

Anna's mother said after a while. 'I'm sure you two girls will have a lot of catching up to do.' She smiled. 'Anna will probably go on and on about this new boyfriend of hers. Oh, I forgot. You've met him, haven't you Lauren? What did you think of him?'

'He's . . . he's very nice,' Lauren answered, trying to sound normal, thinking, how am I going to cope with all of this?

'I'm hoping to meet him soon, too. He sounds wonderful. Well, goodnight girls. I hope you sleep all right, Lauren. You look a bit tired. Don't keep her up too late, Anna.'

'I'll try not to.' Anna smiled, 'but you know what it's like when we get chatting.'

Anna made another cup of coffee and they took it into the lounge and relaxed on the sofa.

'Do you really like Glenn, Lauren? You always sound a bit reserved when we talk about him. I'd hate it if you didn't. Have you got some doubts about him? You'd tell me if you had, wouldn't you?'

'Of course I would,' Lauren lied. She'd known this meeting was going to be tricky, but now she knew her acting abilities were going to be stretched to the limit.

'You see, I've no idea what Glenn feels for me,' Anna went on. 'I think I've been too reserved with him and maybe given the wrong impression. He's always the perfect gentleman when he's with me . . . not that I want him to be anything else, of course . . . but I can't help comparing him with Rob, who was so . . . so passionate and . . . ' Anna went on and on.

All Lauren could think was, my head's still aching and I don't want to hear any of this. She tried to concentrate on what was being said, longing for the time when she could escape from all this pretence.

'I'm sure it's not that Glenn is shy,' Anna was saying, 'but maybe he doesn't find me attractive? Then why does he want to go out with me? Oh, Lauren, I'm in such a muddle. Glenn's so good-looking, so self assured and confident, that I keep thinking, what does he see in me? I'm just ordinary in comparison.'

'Don't belittle yourself, Anna.'

'I'm not. I'm being realistic. He could have any woman he wanted. Somebody more attractive.' She paused. 'Someone like you would be far more suitable.'

'Don't be silly,' Lauren said.

'So,' Anna said, 'have you met anyone nice since you've been home from the Bahamas?'

'No, I'm not looking.' That was true. She didn't have to lie about that.

'When I see Glenn, I'll ask him if he has any nice friends in England who might be suitable for you. How about that?'

'No! Don't do that!' Lauren cried. Then, more calmly, she added, 'That won't be necessary.'

Anna looked questioningly at her

friend. 'What does that mean? Is there someone you're interested in?'

'No, of course not. I just don't want anybody trying to match-make for me, that's all. I'm quite happy as I am.'

'All right. Sorry. I was only trying to help.'

'I know you were.' Lauren felt guilty for being sharp with her friend. 'Look, I really do feel tired and I've still got this awful headache, Anna, so is it OK if I go to bed?'

'Yes, of course. Sorry about your headache, you should have said. Thanks for listening to me going on and on about Glenn. But talking to you has helped me clarify my feelings for him. Goodnight, then, Lauren. I hope you sleep well.'

So do I, Lauren thought, but she doubted it.

She went back home the next day. She knew now that whatever Glenn said, she would have to forget him. When he phoned her again, she would make it clear to him that there could never be anything between them. It would be very hard for her, but that was how it had to be.

* * *

That night, as she was preparing for bed, the phone rang. She thought it would be Anna checking to see if she had arrived home safely.

'Hi Lauren, it's Glenn.'

'Oh, I wasn't expecting to hear from you yet,' she said, her heart pounding.

'You don't make a guy feel very welcome.'

'Sorry, but I was expecting it to be Anna. Where are you?'

'I'm home in Manhattan, but only briefly. Next I'm off to Washington. Then I hope to be in London for a few days. I wanted to speak to you. I've missed you Lauren. I can't wait to see you again.'

'Don't say that.'

'Why not?'

'Because . . . because you should be

saying that to Anna.'

'Lauren, I've told you, it's all over between us.'

'But you haven't told her.'

'No. I haven't had a chance.'

'Glenn, Anna's in love with you. You can't finish with her.'

'But I don't love her. I've told you that. Besides, I think you've got it wrong. She's always so cool with me.

'I think she's still hankering after her former fiancé . . . Rob, wasn't it?'

'Glenn, I've been with her this weekend and I know she's in love with you. She got over Rob a long time ago. Whatever makes you think she's still interested in him?'

'Just things she's said. Anyway, it's you I love, Lauren.'

'No, you don't. It was all a fairytale, Glenn. Just a holiday romance.' She felt as if her heart would break, but she had to say this, for her friend's sake.

'It wasn't just that, and you know it. You know you have feelings for me.'

'It doesn't matter what I feel, Glenn.

It's all over between us. It has to be,' Lauren whispered, trying not to burst into tears.

'You can't say that,' he said desperately. 'Just hold on for a few days and I'll be over. We'll sort things out.'

'No. We can't. Please don't get in touch with me again. We have to make a clean break. We've got to do it for Anna's sake.'

'But I don't love Anna.'

'But she loves you. So you have to forget me.'

'But I can't. I remember every minute we spent together.'

'It wasn't the real world,' Lauren choked. 'We just got carried away by the circumstances. We don't really love each other. We can't. Look, I've got to go.'

'No! You can't! Please, Lauren. Please don't do this to me.'

'I'm sorry Glenn, but it has to be this way.'

'So you don't love me?'

'No.' Lauren felt her heart breaking

even as she said it. She hated lying to Glenn, but she knew it was the only way she would ever get him to give up on her.

'Right, if that's the way things are, I guess there's no point in saying any more.' He sounded dejected and defeated.

'I'm sorry,' Lauren whispered, and put the phone down before the tears came.

She threw herself on to the sofa and sobbed bitterly. She hated herself for what she'd done, but knew there had been no alternative. She'd given her friend a chance of happiness, and that was the important thing. In time she'd get over Glenn, and fortunately for her, he and Anna would be living in Nassau or New York, so she wouldn't have to see them together. She'd throw herself into her job, maybe get a higher position. She was still young. Life would have to get better. That was what Lauren told herself as she lay in bed that night trying to sleep.

★ ★ ★

Lauren returned to the office on Monday, determined to throw herself into work.

'Did you have a good weekend?' one of her colleagues asked.

'Yes thank you,' she lied. 'Lovely.'

'What did you do?'

'Visited a friend.'

'That sounds nice.'

'It was. How was your weekend?' Lauren made polite conversation for a few minutes before walking over to survey her desk.

There was a mountain of documents already heaped up waiting to be dealt with, as well as endless emails. Lauren sat down and started sorting through the pile, sifting out the most urgent looking ones to be dealt with first. Then she tackled the emails. She was glad to be busy.

The day passed quickly and Lauren stayed late to catch up. She was so tired when she arrived home that she just made herself a sandwich and went straight to bed.

The next day she felt much brighter and more energetic after a good night's sleep. She was extremely busy, but Lauren coped well and soon her desk was clear. During the morning, her boss came over to her. 'Lauren, could you come into my office for a moment, please?'

She followed Brian Reynolds into his office, wondering why he wanted to see her. Had she done something wrong? Was she in trouble? She hoped not. She'd always worked hard and done her best, even though hers wasn't the most exciting job in the world. Brian didn't often single her out for special attention.

'Sit down, please, Lauren,' he said now.

'Yes Mr Reynolds?' She looked enquiringly at him.

'Call me Brian, please, and don't look so worried. I've been very pleased with your work.

'You're always calm and efficient and well turned out. You make few mistakes . . . in fact, you're an asset to the company.'

'Thank you Mr . . . er . . . Brian.' This was a surprise. Her boss had hardly spoken to her before. All his praise was usually directed towards her colleagues. She'd always believed that she was much too lowly to be noticed by him.

'So, I was thinking that your hard work deserves recognition,' he went on.

Was he going to give her a rise? That would be good, thought Lauren. I could do with some more money after the amount I spent on that disastrous holiday to the Bahamas.

'So what I was thinking was, how would you like to come on my next business trip to New York?'

'New York?' she gasped. That was where Glenn was. Oh, she didn't want to think about him now.

'Yes, I have to go there for an important meeting in a few days. I need someone to deal with my emails and to take notes at the meeting. I thought you'd fit the bill. Well, what do you say?'

'Me? New York? But why?'

'As I said, I've got to go there on business and I need someone to accompany me. I thought it would be nice for you to come along.'

'I . . . I don't know what to say.'

'Well, I hope you're going to say yes.'

'But what about your secretary? Won't she expect to go?'

'Miss Brown will be on holiday.'

'Oh, I see.' So that was why he wanted her to go. She made up her mind. 'Then of course I'll come, if you're sure I'll be able to cope.'

'Thank you. And don't belittle yourself. I know you'll manage admirably.'

Hadn't she told Anna not to belittle herself the other day, Lauren mused. But don't think about that now, she warned herself. That was in the past. Now you must concentrate on the future. But New York, that was where Glenn was at this very moment. Of all the places in the world, it had to be there!

Lauren's mind was in a whirl for the rest of the day. She'd always wanted to go to New York, and at any other time she'd have been ecstatic. But now, because of her futile feelings of love for a man she could never have, she seemed to be seeing everything through a thick fog. Snap out of it, she told herself. Concentrate on the future; forget about your trip to Nassau.

But that was impossible.

* * *

Just before she left the office, Brian gave Lauren her itinerary. She studied it when she got home and realised she only had three days to prepare. Would Glenn have left New York by then, or would he still be there? He'd said he was going to Washington afterwards, hadn't he? Forget him, she ordered herself once again.

Lauren made a great effort at sorting her wardrobe, picking out the most appropriate business-like clothes, as well as more casual ones for any sightseeing there might be time for, and something more formal in case there were any evening functions to attend.

Lauren phoned her brother and he was delighted for her. 'New York!' he exclaimed. 'You've always wanted to go there. How brilliant! You're a lucky girl, aren't you?'

'Yes I am,' she agreed, trying hard to sound excited.

'You'll have to tell me all about it when you get back. Jo will be green with envy. She's always talking about going to New York one day.'

'You'll probably get fed up with hearing about it,' Lauren replied, knowing that was what her brother would have expected her to say. She didn't want him to know about the turmoil going on inside her.

The day before the trip Lauren still

hadn't heard from Anna. She phoned her friend, but there was no reply. She guessed that Anna was at the hospital. She left a message, saying she'd be in touch when she got back.

A Memorable Trip

Lauren met her boss, Brian, at the airport. She thought it was strange to see him dressed in a lightweight, but expensive-looking, beige suit. He looked so much younger and more approachable somehow. In the office he always wore very formal, dark clothes.

'It's lovely to see you,' he greeted her, shaking her hand. 'You look very nice. Let me take your suitcase.'

He picked up her case and marched ahead of Lauren to the check-in desk. She felt glad that she'd worn her new, blue jacket and matching skirt with toning shoes and handbag. At least Brian approves of this outfit, she thought. I hope the rest of my clothes will be suitable.

As they waited at the desk, she couldn't help remembering that the last time she had been at the airport she had been on her way to Nassau. So much had happened since then, it was hard to believe it was such a short time ago. Her brother had seen her off on that occasion, but this time he'd been too busy. He'd been very apologetic, but she'd assured him that she could manage on her own. 'Besides, I'll be meeting my boss there, so I won't be alone for long.'

'What's he like? Will you be all right with him on your own?' Michael had said, in his protective big-brother way.

'He's OK, always very formal. I'll be quite safe. You won't have to worry about me.'

'How old is he?'

'About forty-five, I should think. It's hard to tell, really. Too old for me, if that's what you're thinking.'

'But it's strange that he asked you, isn't it? What about his secretary?'

'She's going to be away on holiday.'

'Oh, I suppose it's all right then.'

'Of course it is. I'm a big girl now,

Michael. I can take care of myself. So stop worrying. I'll ring you when we've arrived.'

* * *

Lauren was impressed when Brian escorted her to the Business Class lounge, where a buffet breakfast was provided free of charge, along with many other facilities, such as a library area, a massage treatment room and free magazines and newspapers. 'It's wonderful,' she gasped.

'I'm glad you like it,' he grinned.

She enjoyed the flight to New York. Her boss had booked them into Business Class and the service on board was superb. Lauren marvelled at the reclining beds, the personal televisions and the bag full of toiletries, as well as the attention which was given to them by the staff. 'The food's wonderful,' she told Brian. 'it's like a five star restaurant.'

'Not quite,' he laughed, 'but it's

certainly better than economy. I'll have to take you to a five-star hotel one day, then you'll see the difference.'

Lauren couldn't think what to reply to that. Her boss didn't usually treat his staff to meals at five-star restaurants.

'I'm so glad you could come on this trip,' he said.

'Yes, so am I,' Lauren murmured. Suddenly she realised it was true. 'I just hope I'll be able to cope.'

'Of course you will. I've every confidence in you. Anyway, it won't be all work. We'll be able to do quite a bit of sightseeing, too. I think you'll like New York.'

'I'm sure I will.'

* * *

On their arrival at the airport, Brian hailed a yellow taxi cab and they were soon on their way to their hotel. Lauren was surprised that there were no skyscrapers.

'You'll see some soon enough when

we get to Manhattan,' Brian told her.

He had booked two adjoining rooms in a smart hotel near Fifth Avenue. Lauren was delighted with the accommodation, revelling in the luxurious surroundings. 'It's lovely,' she said, when Brian showed her around. 'I've never stayed anywhere like this before.'

'I'm glad you like it. It's a good, four star Hotel. Business expenses wouldn't run to a five star one, but we should be comfortable enough here.'

'I'll be more than comfortable,' she assured Brian.

'Now I suggest you have a rest for a while, do some unpacking and get settled in. Then I'll pick you up at about six for dinner. We don't want a late night as we've got a busy day tomorrow. How does that sound?'

'Fine,' Lauren replied.

Two hours later, Brian knocked at her door. 'You look lovely,' he told Lauren. She was pleased that she'd put on one of her newer dresses.

He escorted her down the long

corridor into the lift and past Reception.

Brian went outside and beckoned to a taxi driver. He helped Lauren inside the cab, and a few minutes later they stopped outside a Chinese restaurant. 'I've been here before and the food is always excellent.' He hesitated, 'You do like Chinese, Lauren? I'm sorry, I forgot to ask. If you don't like it, we could always go somewhere else.'

'I love it,' she affirmed.

They spent a pleasant evening. Lauren relaxed and began to enjoy herself. Brian told her about the various meetings they would be attending and what would be expected of her. He did his best to convince her that she was more than capable of fulfilling her duties. 'You'll be fine, so stop worrying.'

They returned to the hotel shortly after nine o'clock, which Lauren calculated would be two o'clock in London. 'Goodnight. I hope you sleep well,' Brian said, as they reached her door.

She lay tossing and turning for a

while, her head buzzing with all the events of the past few days. She was excited to be in New York, but at the back of her mind was the thought, is Glenn still here? Wouldn't it be awful if we bumped into him? No, it would be wonderful, another side of her brain told her, but most unlikely. New York is a huge place. It would be a miracle to spot him here amongst all the myriad of people going about their business. Or has Glenn returned to England, she asked herself? And has he seen Anna yet? But whatever Glenn is doing, it's no concern of yours, she reminded herself.

The next morning, Lauren made herself look as business-like as possible. She was ready when Brian came to collect her. 'Did you sleep well?' he asked.

'Yes, not too badly,' she replied. 'I always find it difficult to sleep in a strange bed.'

'Yes. I know the feeling. I spend quite a bit of time away from home, and not all hotel beds are conducive to a good night's rest.'

Lauren hadn't thought much about her boss's frequent business trips. She wondered if he had a wife and whether she minded him going away so much.

Almost as if he knew what she was thinking, Brian said, 'It's a good thing I've been living on my own recently, a wife might get fed up with my busy schedule.

'But I've decided to cut back on some of my trips. Let someone else go for a change.'

'Yes,' Lauren said. 'That sounds like a good idea.'

* * *

Lauren found the meetings very interesting. Taking notes for her boss gave a different perspective on the telecom business. She'd always quietly tackled the jobs in hand, never taking much notice of what other people in the industry were doing. Now, though, when she got home from America, she'd see if there was any chance of becoming a personal assistant. After all, that was what she was doing on this trip.

Maybe she'd be brave enough to ask Brian what he thought.

She wouldn't do it now, though, she'd wait until they were back at work. See how she got on while she was in New York first. She'd become a career woman. That was what she'd do.

At least then she'd have success in one area of her life. It certainly wasn't going to be in marriage.

That wasn't going to happen . . . ever.

⋆ ⋆ ⋆

Brian had to make several presentations. Lauren was amazed at how comfortably and confidently he talked to large groups of people. He looked so much at ease, showing no sign of nerves, and she had to admire him for this. Everyone at the meetings greeted him favourably, and Lauren felt proud to be working for him.

As Brian had said, it wasn't all work. Each evening they would dine in a different restaurant and discuss the day's events. He seemed very pleased with the contribution Lauren had made. They'd also found time to visit Central Park, which, in spite of the hot weather, she found to be a pleasant and attractive place. But she couldn't help feeling envious of all the young lovers strolling hand in hand, aware only of each other. Was that what Anna and Glenn were doing now, she wondered? Had Anna told him how she felt? Had Glenn forgotten her already?

'Lauren?'

She realised that Brian was speaking.

'I'm sorry,' Lauren murmured. 'What did you say?'

'I was just asking if you had a boyfriend.'

'Oh no,' she answered quickly, her face flushing profusely. Now why was he asking that, she thought. So far, all their conversations had been very professional and business-like. She didn't want to get on to more personal things. 'This park is wonderful,' she exclaimed, changing the subject before he could pursue the topic.

'Yes it is,' Brian replied, staring at her with a strange expression on his face that unnerved her, making her look away. 'Tomorrow's our last day,' he went on. 'We only have one short meeting in the morning, so I suggest we spend the rest of the time sightseeing. What do you say to that?'

'Lovely,' Lauren replied.

* * *

That night she had a weird dream causing her to wake with a start. She kept seeing Glenn, Anna and Brian shut up together in a lift that was stuck between floors. They were calling for her to help them, but when she tried to, she couldn't. Her legs seemed to be stuck in quicksand, and every time she moved, she just got deeper into it.

'Help!' she cried out, waking herself up.

She looked around the room, terror being replaced with relief as she realised it was only a dream. I hope no-one heard me, she thought, feeling rather foolish for crying out in her sleep.

Suddenly she could hear a gentle but persistent tapping on her door. 'Lauren . . . Lauren, are you all right?'

It was Brian.

How embarrassing, Lauren thought, waking her boss up with her screaming! She quickly pulled on a robe, went to the door, opened it slightly and looked out. Brian was standing there in his dressing gown, a look of concern on his face.

'I'm sorry if I woke you up,' Lauren said, her face flaming. 'I must have been having a nightmare.'

'It sounded pretty bad to me. Are you sure you're OK?'

'Yes . . . yes thank you.'

'Do you want to talk about it?'

'No. I've forgotten it already.' That wasn't true. She could still see Glenn and Anna together, but she couldn't tell Brian that.

'You were crying. You sounded really distressed. Do you often have bad nightmares?'

'Sometimes,' she lied.

'Well if you're sure you're all right, I'll go back to bed.' He hesitated. 'Unless . . . would you like a drink or something first?'

'No thank you. I'll be fine now. And . . . thanks, Brian, for your concern. I'll see you in the morning.'

'OK. Goodnight then, Lauren.'

* * *

The next morning, after their last meeting, Brian suggested, 'How about a coffee and cheesecake before we get down to some serious sightseeing? Unless of course you want something more substantial?'

'No that would be lovely,' Lauren replied. 'I love New York cheesecake. And I had a good breakfast, so that will keep me going until tonight.'

'Good. We'll have dinner somewhere really swish for our last evening.'

* * *

As they sat drinking their coffee, Brian asked, 'Have you enjoyed the trip, Lauren?'

'Very much.'

'Well, I hope that this will be the first of many.'

'But you'll have to take Miss Brown next time.'

'She won't always be my secretary. In fact, she's getting married in a few months and has told me that she'll be moving away from London. Of course it's not official yet, so I'd be grateful if you didn't say anything.'

'No, I won't say a word. But I didn't know she was even engaged.'

'The thing is, I was wondering,

Lauren, if you might consider working for me as my personal assistant? You don't have to decide now, but I'd like you to think about it. I've been very pleased with your work and you've coped admirably on this trip. We're a good team. We get on well together.'

'Oh,' Lauren gasped. 'I don't know what to say.'

'As I said, you don't have to decide now. There's plenty of time.'

* * *

They spent the rest of the day wandering around New York, visiting Broadway, Times Square, looking in shop windows in Fifth Avenue, and going up to the top of the Empire State Building.

Lauren noticed how relaxed and friendly Brian had become towards her, so different from the stiff and starchy man she saw in the office, but she guessed that once they arrived home, he'd revert to his more formal ways. He laughed and joked so much that she found it hard to remember that he was her boss.

At the back of her mind was the thought that, if she were successful in getting Miss Brown's job, she would be going on many more trips with Brian. That would be the answer to all her problems. Hadn't she been contemplating becoming a career woman? But she wouldn't worry about that now. She'd just enjoy this last evening.

Suddenly she remembered her final evening in Nassau, and how she'd been feeling then. She quickly thrust those thoughts from her mind. Her time in the Bahamas was a closed book. They were in the past. Now she had to think about the future.

* * *

They dined sumptuously at an exclusive restaurant. Lauren was horrified when she caught sight of the bill. 'Brian,' she exclaimed, 'you shouldn't have spent that much. I'm sure you can't claim that off expenses.'

'No, I wasn't going to. I just felt like treating you. We've had such a good time together, I wanted to reward you.'

'Thank you. I've really enjoyed this trip. I'm so glad you asked me.'

'So am I. I haven't felt this happy for ages.'

Lauren was surprised at this, but then she thought, what do I know about him? I've only seen him in work. I know nothing of his private life. Maybe he's had a tough time, too. I'm not the only one who has problems, I guess.

'Lauren,' she heard him saying.

'Yes, Brian?'

He took hold of her hand and looked at her intently. Whatever was he going to say?

'I was thinking, you and I get on so well, I was wondering . . . if . . . if you'd consider going out with me when we get home, maybe to the theatre or for dinner?'

'Oh,' Lauren gasped. 'Oh, I . . . I . . . '

'I'm sorry,' Brian exclaimed, pulling his hand away. 'I shouldn't have asked.'

'No, that's all right,' Lauren answered quickly. 'I was just surprised.'

'Well, as you said you didn't already have a boyfriend, I thought I'd ask, but of course, if you don't want to, I'll quite understand. I am a lot older than you, but I've become very fond of you during the past few days.'

Lauren could see the look of disappointment on Brian's face. She knew how that felt. She didn't want to upset him, but going out with him wasn't something she'd ever considered. 'I . . . I don't know what to say.'

'Don't answer me now. I can see you're a bit shocked. We'll change the subject, but if you do decide you'd like a night out when we get back home, just let me know. Is that all right?'

'Yes. Yes, thank you.'

* * *

That evening, as Lauren finished packing ready for her homeward journey the next day, she mulled over what Brian had said. She had been utterly amazed at his suggestion. The notion that he might be interested in going out with her had never entered her head. She'd been so pre-occupied with her thoughts about Glenn, she hadn't seen this coming. He'd made comments about being on his own, but she still had no idea as to whether he'd ever been married. If she got the chance, she would have to ask him.

But how was she going to answer his question? Of course she'd have to refuse his offer. But what reason could she give? She didn't want to hurt him. He was a good man, kind and considerate. He didn't deserve to be treated badly. Suddenly she remembered that she'd been having the same thoughts about Anna. She didn't want to hurt her, either. Lauren wondered why it was that she got herself into these situations. Why did she have to continually tread on eggshells, trying not to upset other people? What about my feelings? Where do they come in all of this?

Lauren spent another restless night. At breakfast Brian asked if she'd slept well, but made no allusion to their conversation the evening before.

They were again in Business Class for their return journey. When the stewardess asked Lauren if she'd travelled that way before, she replied airily, 'Oh yes,' as if that was her normal method of travel.

Brian laughed, 'I think you're getting accustomed to this way of life.'

'I think I am,' she smiled.

After they'd settled into their seats and were drinking their complementary glass of champagne, Brian asked, 'Have you given any thought to what I said last night?'

Lauren took a deep breath. 'I still don't know what to say. It was very kind of you to ask me to go out with you, but . . . '

'But you don't fancy me. Is that what it is? I'm too old for you?'

'Er . . . '

'Or you're in love with someone else? Is that it?'

She could feel herself blushing. 'I . . . I . . . '

'Oh, I'm sorry, Lauren, I can see I've hit a nerve. I shouldn't be asking you all these questions. Let's forget what I said.'

'No. I'm the one who should be sorry,' Lauren interrupted, noting the look of disappointment on his face, feeling guilty, knowing she was the cause of it.

'You have nothing to be sorry about. I should be old enough and wise enough not to get myself into these situations. We'll say no more about it. When we get back home, we'll revert to our former roles of boss and employee, but I'll just say one thing, Lauren. My offer of you becoming my personal assistant when Miss Brown leaves still stands.'

'Thank you, Brian.'

'Good. Now have some more champagne.'

They sat quietly for a few minutes, until Lauren could stand the silence no more. 'You were right,' she blurted out.

'Pardon?'

'I said you were right. I am in love with someone else, somebody who I can never have.' Why was she saying this? Was it the champagne that had loosened her tongue?

'I am sorry. I know how that feels.'

'You do?'

'Yes. I might be a lot older than you, but I still have feelings, you know,' he smiled.

'Of course you do. I'm sorry.'

'Do you want to talk about it? It helps sometimes.'

'Nothing can help me. I've just got to get over it.'

'That's what I had to do.'

'And did it work?'

'I think so. I'm over it now.'

'What happened?'

'My . . . my wife left me for someone else. Someone I thought was my friend.'

'Oh, how awful!' Suddenly Lauren could see the parallel between her and Glenn and Anna. She knew she had been right not to give in to Glenn.

She could see how hurt Brian was. She couldn't do that to her friend.

'Don't look so worried. I'm over it now, I told you. And you'll get over it too, if you try. I'm not pretending it's easy, but it is possible.

'At one time I couldn't even bear to say my wife's name, but that doesn't worry me any more.'

'Did you have any children?'

'No. Anyway, that's all in the past. We were divorced five years ago.'

'Brian . . . '

'Yes.'

'If the offer still stands, I'll go out with you.'

'You will? Are you sure that's what you want to do?'

'I think so.'

'You think so?'

'I'm in a muddle, Brian, I'll be honest with you. I fell in love with someone I can never have, because he belongs to someone else, so if you still want to go out with me, knowing that, then I'll do it. No strings, though. Is that clear?'

'It sounds a bit like a business proposition to me, but I'm willing to give it a go. See what happens. After all, I've got nothing to lose . . . only everything to gain.' He took hold of her hand, squeezed it, and said, 'I hope you won't regret this when you get back home.' He hesitated, 'In fact I think it might be better if we don't make any decision now. I'll ask you again when we're back at work. See what you think then. Does that sound fair?'

'Yes, very fair. Thank you, Brian.'

The rest of the journey passed in a blur. Lauren realised that she had drunk too much champagne. She wasn't used to this luxurious living. At the airport, Brian escorted her back home in a black cab. As she got out, he lightly kissed her forehead. 'Goodbye, Lauren. I'll see you in the office tomorrow, and thank you for a wonderful trip.'

'Thank you, Brian.'

She went into her flat, threw her suitcase down and was just about to run a bath when she noticed her answer phone flashing.

She listened to her first message, which was from Anna.

'I've got something to tell you, Lauren,' she said. 'Please ring me back when you get home.'

What was it Anna had to tell her? Was it about her father, or was it about Glenn? Had he proposed? I'll have to phone her tomorrow. I can't face hearing about Glenn now, I'm far too tired to concentrate on anything. I'd probably say all the wrong things, like I did on the aeroplane with Brian. Should I have agreed to go out with him, Laura pondered? Am I being fair? I did tell him how I felt and he didn't seem put off by it, so I have been honest with him.

She pressed the button to hear her second message. Glenn's unmistakable voice filled the room. 'Lauren, I need to talk to you. I know you said it was over between us but I have something important to tell you, which I think you should hear. It could change everything. Please ring me back as soon as you get this message. I'm in London now, but only for another forty-eight hours. If I don't hear from you, I'll know you meant what you said, and that we're finished, and I won't bother you again. But I can't really believe that's what you want. Please reply.'

Anna Drops A Bombshell

Lauren gasped, her heart missing a beat. What does Glenn want to tell me? Could it mean that he's finished with Anna? She said that she has something important to tell me, too, so it must be that. Oh, just when I was contemplating a new life without him, he rings and brings all those old feelings back. Then realisation dawned on her. Forty-eight hours, he said. When did he make that call? Oh no, five days ago, she choked. It's too late to do anything now. He must be back in America. I can't contact him. He thinks I don't care about him. But I do. So very much.

What can I do? How can I get in touch with him? So many questions were going round and round in her head and Lauren couldn't answer any of them. There was nothing she could do at that moment to resolve the situation. She'd have to wait until the next day. She hoped her head would be clearer then, so she'd be able to plan her course of action.

Although she was tired, Lauren tossed and turned. What about Brian? She'd said she would go out with him, but now, if there was just the tiniest, most remote possibility, that she and Glenn might get together, she couldn't do it. She'd have to tell Brian. There seemed to be no satisfactory solutions to any of her problems. Someone would get hurt no matter what she did.

She finally fell into a restless sleep.

Next morning, she arrived punctually at work to be greeted by her colleagues.

'How was your trip to New York?' they asked.

'Fine,' she replied, not wanting to elaborate on the subject.

'What about you know who?' one of the secretaries whispered, pointing in the direction of Brian's office. 'Was he okay? Just as formal as ever?'

'Everything was fine. Now, if you

don't mind, I must get on with my work, I've lots of catching up to do.'

'You can tell us the gory details.'

She forced a smile. 'There's really nothing to tell.'

Lauren hadn't bargained on her work colleagues wanting to know about the trip. Now I've got them to contend with, as well as working out what to say to Brian. And tonight, she had to phone Anna, and then she had to decide what to do about Glenn.

The day dragged on. There was so much to do that Lauren had to stay late. She only caught brief glimpses of Brian as he came out of his office. She didn't look in his direction, just kept her head down and got on with her work.

As she walked out of the building, Brian caught up with her.

'You haven't been avoiding me, have you, Lauren?'

'No, of course not. I . . . I've just been very busy . . . so much catching up to do.'

'I wanted to ask if you'd recovered from the trip.'

'Yes thank you . . . still a bit jet lagged, though, so I'm going home for an early night.'

'All right, I'll leave you in peace. Perhaps we can have a chat tomorrow after work. I'll phone you, if that's okay? It's best not to do it in the office . . . you know . . . tongues might start wagging.'

They were doing that already, Lauren thought. 'Yes, that's fine,' she told Brian.

* * *

What was she going to do about Glenn? That was her main worry as she made her way home from work. How could she get in touch with him? She had no telephone number or home address and she didn't know his email address, either. What had he wanted to say to her that changed everything? Would she be able to reach him at one of his father's hotels? Maybe, but she didn't know the name of any of them, so that was no use.

Lauren opened a tin of soup when she arrived home, and made some toast. She couldn't face anything more elaborate. When she'd finished eating, she phoned Anna, but her line was engaged. She left a message: 'I hope everything is okay with you. I'm going to bed in an hour, still suffering from jet lag, but if you want to ring me back before that you can, or you could send me a text. I hope your father is all right.'

Thirty minutes later, Anna returned her call. 'Sorry, I was on the phone when you called. And you'll never guess who I was talking to!'

'Who?' I suppose it was Glenn, Lauren thought, her heart sinking, but she couldn't bring herself to say his name.

'Rob.'

'Rob!'

'Yes. Oh, Lauren, he's been in touch again.'

'But . . . I thought you didn't want to have anything to do with him?'

'I didn't, but . . . I've changed my mind.'

'You've what?'

'I'm sorry, is this a bad line, Lauren? Can't you hear me?'

'Yes, but I can't believe what I am hearing. After all you've said, you're telling me that . . . that . . . '

'I'm going to see Rob again,' Anna interrupted.

'But . . . but what about Glenn?' Lauren's heart began to beat furiously.

'That's my biggest problem,' Anna said. 'I don't know how to tell him, especially as he was so nice the last time I saw him, very affectionate. In fact, quite different from how he usually is. I've never been sure what his feelings were for me, but, oh, Lauren, I'm worried he might be falling in love with me and I know now that it's Rob I want.

'How am I going to tell Glenn? He went back to America a few days ago, and I'm not sure when I'll see him again. What can I say to him, Lauren?'

Anna thinks Glenn's fallen in love with her; those words were going round and round in her head.

'Lauren? Are you still there?'

'Er . . . yes. Sorry, it's not a very good line,' she lied.

'I was saying that I think Glenn's fallen in love with me, but I don't love him. I'm still in love with Rob.'

'Even after what he did to you? And you've forgiven him?'

'He's apologised. He's really sorry for what he did.'

'And you believe him?'

'Yes. Lauren, please be happy for me. I really do believe he's genuinely sorry.'

'But he could do the same thing to you again. Some men are like that. One woman isn't enough for them.'

'You're thinking of Jake, aren't you?'

'What if I am? I trusted him, but look what happened. I discovered he was already engaged.'

'Rob's not engaged. He wants to

marry me. And I'm sure it will be all right this time. Anyway, it's Glenn I'm worried about. What can I do? I don't want to hurt him. He's been so different recently.'

'In what way?' Lauren asked, thinking, I don't really want to hear all this. But she had no choice, she couldn't hang up on her friend.

'I don't know,' Anna mused. 'He's been more, well, passionate, I suppose. That's what makes me think he's realised he's in love with me. He wasn't like that before. He was always a bit distant.'

So I've been right all along, Lauren thought. Glenn does love Anna. What happened between us was just a fling on his part. But it wasn't on mine. Oh Glenn, I wish I'd never met you.

'Are you still there, Lauren? Can you hear me?'

'Yes, but this line's so bad I think I'd better go.'

'Please don't go, Lauren, I need your advice. I've no idea what to do. Can you suggest anything? How can I tell Glenn I still love Rob?' She paused, then before Lauren could reply, went on, 'It was all like a dream with Glenn. He was so good-looking, so self-assured, that I suppose I was flattered when he asked someone ordinary like me to go out with him. But I think I knew all along it would never work out. And I was never really in love with him. I know that now. So what can I do?'

'I don't know. I'm afraid I can't help you with that,' Lauren answered brusquely, thinking, if only she'd said that weeks ago, I wouldn't have pushed Glenn away. I was trying so hard not to hurt Anna, and now I'm the one who's hurt. 'Anyway, how's your father getting on? You haven't mentioned him.' Lauren was desperate to change the subject.

'He's much better, thanks. Sorry, Lauren, to keep on about my problems. You must be tired after your trip. I'll be over here a few more days yet, but then I'll have to go back to Nassau. I hope that by then Dad will be out of hospital.

'The trouble is, I don't want to go back to the Bahamas now, but I am on a contract, so I've got to.

'Perhaps we can talk another time, or maybe meet? I do need your advice.'

'Yes, we can meet, but my advice wouldn't be worth having, I'm afraid,' Lauren said, thinking, I can't solve my own problems, so how can I be expected to help Anna, especially since the same person is involved in both situations?

'I'm sorry I can't be more helpful,' she said.

'Just listening to me rambling on helps. I'll just have to try and sort something out with Glenn when I see him.'

'When's that?' Lauren asked, her hopes rising for a moment.

If he comes back soon, perhaps I could ring him, she thought, but then they were dashed as she remembered that Anna had said Glenn was in love with her.

'As I said, I've no idea,' Anna replied. 'That's always been the problem. I never know when I'm going to see him. He can be so elusive.'

'It's his job,' Lauren blurted out.

'You're right, of course. I should be more understanding. Still, I'm surprised at you for defending him. I had a feeling you didn't like him.'

'Look Anna, I must go, I'm nearly falling asleep,' Lauren yawned.

'Okay, I won't keep you any longer. Thanks for listening to me.'

* * *

The next day after work, Brian phoned to ask if Lauren had thought about what he had said about them going out together.

'I'm sorry, Brian, but I've been so busy at work and at home I haven't had time to think.' She knew that sounded a bit feeble, but she didn't know what else to say.

'Oh,' he replied. 'I take it that means

you don't want to go out with me.'

'No. I'm just not sure,' she answered, not wanting to hurt his feelings. 'I . . . I . . . '

'That's all right,' he interrupted, 'you don't have to answer now, but the offer still stands. If you fancy a night out any time, I'd be pleased to go with you. Just let me know. And, for the record, if you do decide that you'd rather not go out with me, you won't lose your chance of promotion, so don't worry on that score. How does that sound?'

'Very fair, Brian, thank you.' Lauren felt terrible. 'You're very kind.' Should she go out with him once, just to be sociable? She really didn't know what to do.

'I won't keep you any longer. Bye Lauren,' Brian said, and hung up, before she could make any reply.

* * *

Two days later, Anna invited Lauren to visit her. She didn't want to go, but could think of no way of getting out of it. She knew that she'd be in for a difficult time with Anna constantly going on about Glenn and Rob. However, if it was true that Anna wanted to finish with Glenn, there was still a glimmer of hope that maybe . . . just maybe . . . there was a chance for her.

She decided to go at the weekend and see what Anna had to say.

* * *

'It's so lovely to see you again,' Anna said, as she hugged Lauren. 'My mother's at the hospital. There's afternoon visiting on a Saturday, so we can have a chat before she comes back.

'How was your trip to America? I'm sorry, but in all my excitement at hearing from Rob again, I forgot to ask.'

'It was fine, thanks.'

'What's your boss like? Is he married? What's his name? Was it all right just going with him? He didn't try anything, did he, Lauren?'

'It's Brian, and no, he's not married, he's divorced.'

'Divorced?'

'He's very respectable,' Lauren said. 'And no, he didn't try anything. He was the perfect gentleman. Besides, he's a lot older than me.'

'Age doesn't matter.'

'I know it doesn't, but . . . '

'So you're not interested in him?'

'No, I'm not. Brian's a very nice person and a good boss, but that's all.' Lauren wasn't going to tell Anna that he had asked her to go out with him. She'd never hear the end of it if she did. 'Now you tell me about Rob,' she forced herself to say.

'There's not much else to tell. I haven't seen him yet, but I will in a few days. He lives in Manchester now. Got a job there. He's been busy settling into his new flat. He's coming to see me next weekend. And I can't wait!'

'What made him get in touch with

you again? I thought you'd told him you didn't want any more to do with him?'

'I did, but that was over a year ago.'

'What about Glenn?' Lauren forced herself to sound normal as she said the words. She could feel herself flinching and hoped Anna hadn't noticed. She needn't have worried, though. Anna was too starry-eyed to notice anything.

'I thought maybe I was in love with Glenn,' Anna replied, 'but then Rob phoned, and as soon as I heard his voice, I knew it was him I loved.'

'What made him phone?'

'I don't know, really. He just said that he suddenly felt the need to do it. It was almost like Fate, because if he hadn't rung then, the next time I saw Glenn I might have told him I loved him, and I know now that wouldn't have been true.'

'Oh.' Lauren couldn't think what else to say.

'It all seems as if it was meant to be,' Anna went on. 'You see, Rob couldn't have known that I would be at my mother's house when he rang, but I was, almost as if I was waiting for his call. Does that sound silly, Lauren?'

'No.' It didn't sound silly at all. In fact she might have agreed with Anna that it was meant to be, except for the one fact, that Glenn was in love with Anna, not her. She couldn't get that out of her head.

'What am I going to do about Glenn'? Anna continued. 'I don't want to hurt him, but if he is in love with me, how can I tell him I love Rob?'

Just a short time ago, Lauren mused, she'd been worrying about how to tell Anna that she and Glenn were in love. How the tables had turned! 'I . . . I don't know,' was all she could answer.

'If only Glenn didn't love me,' Anna sighed.

If only, Lauren thought.

'I don't think I can hurt him,' Anna said. 'He doesn't deserve it.'

'No, but if you love someone else, you'll have to tell him.' Didn't Glenn say this to her about Anna? 'When are you going to see him again?'

'I still don't know. I've no idea where he is. Oh, let's change the subject. This is getting me nowhere, and it must be very boring for you. I'll just have to play it by ear and see what happens when we meet again. Perhaps I've got it all wrong and he's not in love with me. I hope that is the case.'

So do I, Lauren echoed in her heart.

* * *

They spent the next half-hour chatting about other things. Suddenly the doorbell rang. 'I wonder who that can be?' Anna said. 'I don't think it's Mum. She always takes her key.'

She went into the hall and opened the door.

'Oh . . . oh . . . hello,' Lauren heard her saying.

'Hi Anna, it's so good to see you again. Can I come in?

'You're looking as if you've seen a

ghost. Aren't you pleased to see me?'

Lauren heard the voice with horror. She wanted to run out of the door, but couldn't move. What was she going to do?

Glenn was here.

'We're not on our own,' Lauren heard Anna murmur.

'We're not? Never mind. Surely a guy can kiss his girlfriend, to show how pleased he is to see her? Anyway, who's here?'

'It's Lauren.'

'What . . . what's she doing here?'

Lauren could hear the tightness in his voice. 'Get rid of her,' he muttered. 'I've come to see you.'

'Shush Glenn, she'll hear you,' Anna chided.

'I don't care if she does. She's the last person I expected to see.'

'Well you'll have to come and say hello to her. It would be very rude not to.'

Anna dragged Glenn into the lounge. 'What a surprise! I'd no idea Glenn was over here,' she said, turning to Lauren, whose face was turning crimson with embarrassment and anger. How dare he, she thought. All that time I'd believed he felt something for me, and now I can see it was all a sham.

'I'd better go,' Lauren said, hardly glancing at Glenn. 'Goodbye, Anna. I'll be in touch.' She grabbed her bag and went towards the door, but Glenn was standing in her way.

'Hello, Lauren.' His voice sounded cold as ice. 'What are you doing here?'

'I . . . I came to see my friend.'

'You don't have to go on account of me,' he said, staring at Lauren, who, despite her feelings of anger and confusion, couldn't resist gazing into his eyes. How hard they look today, she thought, so different from when he . . .

'Stay a bit longer,' Anna implored. 'I'd like it if you did.'

'No, I really must go. Don't bother to see me out. Bye.'

Lauren fled through the door before they could stop her. She hurried down the road and round the corner, then collapsed, breathless, on to a bench at a nearby bus stop. As she sat there, she began to regret her actions. Why had she run off like a frightened rabbit? She should have stayed and brazened it out. Anna hadn't wanted her to go. And Glenn . . . what had he wanted? Not her, that was for sure. He'd been kissing her and flirting with her, when he was supposed to be Anna's boyfriend. It had all been an act, pretending he cared about her, when all the time, he was just amusing himself, behind Anna's back. I hope Anna's had enough sense to finish with Glenn and tell him about Rob, she thought. It's no more than he deserves. She's well rid of him.

* * *

Lauren travelled back, pondering over the events of the afternoon. By the time she arrived home, she'd made a decision. She would accept Brian's offer. She felt glad that at last she had seen Glenn for what he was, a philanderer. Now she could put that episode of her life behind her and concentrate on the future. What if Brian was a lot older? Did it matter? No, of course it didn't. She'd go out with him and see what transpired.

The next day, Lauren received a phone call from Anna. 'I'm sorry about last night,' her friend said. 'I'd no idea Glenn was over here. That was a total surprise. You see, that's always been my problem. I never know where I am with him or when I'm going to see him. But you didn't have to rush off like that, Lauren. You could have stayed longer. My mum wondered why you'd gone so early.'

'It was best that I did. You know what they say about three being a crowd,' Lauren joked. 'Besides, you needed to talk to Glenn. You couldn't have done that if I was there.

'So . . . did you tell him about Rob?'

'No, I didn't actually. It was all very difficult.'

'Difficult? How?'

'I tried to tell him, but he seemed so pleased to see me that I couldn't bring myself to do it. He was . . . so, well . . . loving.'

'Oh, Anna.' Lauren tried to stop visions of Glenn coming into her mind, kissing Anna passionately, the way he'd kissed her.

'I know I should have told Glenn, but I just couldn't hurt him.'

Lauren forced herself to say, 'But if you're going to see Rob again, you'll have to tell him.'

'I know, but I'll have to try and lead up to it somehow, so that I let him down gently.'

Lauren wanted to shout at Anna, 'Don't worry about upsetting him, he's not worth it! He's just a philanderer!' But how could she say that, without revealing what had happened when Anna was away in England, and Lauren was in Nassau?

Instead, she mumbled, 'You'll have to do what you think best.'

'You don't have a good opinion of Glenn, do you?' Anna commented.

'What I think is irrelevant,' Lauren replied. 'It's what you do, that's important.'

'That's not an answer. I knew right from the beginning you didn't like Glenn, but I've never been able to figure out why?'

'I have never said that I didn't like Glenn.'

'No, but you've implied it.'

'Well, I'm sorry if I did. I didn't mean to. Anyway, that's all beside the point now. You've got to find a way of telling him about Rob.'

'I know. I will do it, but I've got to find the right time. Thanks for listening to me, Lauren. Just talking things over helps. I'll do the same for you one day.'

After a brief update on her father, Anna hung up,' and Lauren breathed a sigh of relief. But now what, she thought?

She sank down onto the sofa. It was

bizarre how everything had turned out. She had fallen in love with Glenn but had rejected his advances, because she thought Anna loved him, when all the time, it was Glenn who was in love with Anna. So where did she come in the equation, Lauren asked herself? Nowhere, she decided.

* * *

After work on Monday, Lauren phoned Brian. They chatted for a short time about work and then Lauren said, 'Does your offer still stand?'

'You mean about going on a . . . a date?'

'Yes.'

'Of course it does, but I'm surprised. I thought you didn't want to go out with me.'

'It wasn't that. I was just a bit . . . '

'You don't have to justify yourself to me, Lauren. So why don't we have dinner next Saturday? See how we get on? Then we can take it from there. No strings. What do you think?'

'Sounds fine to me.'

Lauren hung up, wondering if she'd done the right thing. Do I really want to go out with Brian?' she asked herself. Won't I end up comparing him with Glenn? No, they're entirely different people. Anyway, we're just going out as friends, nothing more. He's on his own and so am I. What harm is there in us getting together? I don't want to sit at home alone, moping over Glenn.

* * *

Lauren had little contact with Brian at work until Friday evening, when she was busy tidying her desk. He walked over to her and said in a low voice, 'Are we still on for tomorrow?'

'Yes,' she replied quietly.

'Good. I'm looking forward to it. I'll pick you up at seven.'

Going out with your boss can be quite tricky, Lauren thought, having to watch your step all the time, to make sure you haven't done anything indiscreet. Then she smiled to herself. I'm going out with him for the first time tomorrow, and that will probably be the last, so what am I worrying about?

The next day, Lauren dithered around, trying to decide what to wear for the evening. She guessed that they'd be going to an expensive restaurant, and she didn't want to look out of place. On the other hand, she didn't want to look too dressed up, in case Brian got the wrong idea.

In the end, she chose a peach two-piece outfit which fitted her perfectly. She'd washed and brushed her long hair until it gleamed. She was looking forward to having an evening out, but at the same time, was nervous about it. What would they talk about? Work? That wouldn't be very interesting. She told herself to stop being silly. She'd just come back from a few days in New York with Brian, and they'd got on perfectly well then, so why shouldn't they now? But that was different, she argued. They were there on business. This was a date. You don't have to go, she kept telling herself, but knew it was too late to change her mind, so decided she'd just have to make the best of it.

* * *

Brian arrived on time at seven o'clock. Lauren was ready. 'You look very nice,' he told her, as he stood in the doorway.

'Thank you,' she replied, picking up her handbag and closing the door.

'My car's a little way down the road. It's busy round here,' Brian said.

'Yes it's always hard to find a parking space,' Lauren agreed.

Lauren followed Brian as he led her towards his car. They had only walked a few yards when a large black saloon pulled up a short distance in front of them. The door was thrust open and a tall man jumped out. 'Lauren!' he exclaimed. 'Where are you going? I was just coming round to see you. We've got some sorting out to do and we need to do it now.'

'Glenn,' she said, her face ashen.

Lauren Is In Turmoil

'I'm sorry Glenn, I'm going out with . . . ' Brian held out his hand. 'Hello. I'm Brian. I'm Lauren's boss.'

Brian quickly took charge of the situation. 'You need to talk to Lauren now you say? Is it urgent? We're just on our way into town for dinner.'

'Her . . . her boss? And she's having dinner with you?'

'That's right. And you are?'

'Er . . . me, I'm Glenn. Lauren's having dinner with you?' he repeated.

'Yes, as I just told you. Now, Glenn, is it important? We do have to get going.'

'No. Well, yes. Well . . . I wanted to sort things out with her now.' He turned to Lauren. 'Can we talk?'

'Not . . . not now.' Why was this happening? She'd never imagined this scenario, Glenn turning up, just as she was about to go out with Brian. What must her boss be thinking? 'Tomorrow? Is that any good?' she asked in a small voice.

'I suppose it can wait till then,' Glenn said, staring intently at her.

Lauren had never seen him lost for words before. Although she was mortified at meeting Glenn in this way, she couldn't help admiring the confident manner in which Brian had handled him. He was the self-assured one now, not Glenn.

'Good, so if you make your arrangements, we'll be on our way,' Brian said.

'Yes . . . well . . . I guess it'll have to be tomorrow then, only I fly back to New York on Monday.'

'I'm home all day,' Lauren confirmed, feeling secretly pleased at witnessing the discomfiture on Glenn's face. She quite enjoyed the experience of having the upper hand. 'Do you want to ring me?' she said.

'I was hoping to see you.'

'Oh. Is that necessary? Can't you say

whatever you want to say over the phone?'

Was she really saying this to Glenn? Where had this new-found courage come from? She wanted to see him desperately, but she wasn't going to let him know that. She just hoped he couldn't hear her heart thumping madly.

'No, I can't say it over the phone,' he told her.

'You'd better come round after lunch, then.'

'OK.'

'Right. See you then. Let's go, Brian.'

'Nice to meet you Glenn,' Brian said, as he took Lauren's arm and guided her towards his car. She didn't look round, but she sensed Glenn was staring after them.

When she got into the car, the full impact of what had happened hit her. The thought, *Glenn wants to see me* kept going round and round in her head. Why? What was he going to say? Had Anna told him about Rob? If she had, the only reason he'd want to see her again, would be because . . . because he . . .

'It won't take long to get to the restaurant,' Brian said, breaking into her thoughts. 'And then you can tell me all about it, if you want to. I gather that was the chap you told me about, the one you were in love with, who belonged to someone else. Am I right?'

'How did you know?'

'It was written all over your face.'

If her feelings were that obvious to Brian, did Glenn, too, realise that she'd been bluffing when she played it cool with him?

'I'm sorry, Brian, this was the last thing I wanted to happen tonight,' she said.

'You don't have to apologise. You told me right from the start that you were in love with someone else.'

'Thanks, Brian, for being so understanding.'

'Anyway, I hope this won't spoil our evening together.'

'No, I won't let it.'

They'd arrived at a car park outside a very exclusive restaurant. Brian had booked a table in a cosy alcove, with a window overlooking a well-stocked garden, where a profusion of dahlias and early chrysanthemums were coming into bloom. 'It's lovely here,' Lauren commented, mustering up as much enthusiasm as she could.

'I'm glad you like it.'

The waiter brought them the menu, which she perused while Brian ordered their drinks. When they were waiting for their starter to arrive, he said, 'Now, do you want to tell me about it? Talking to a friend often helps. And I'd like to think that I am a friend, not just your boss.'

'Thank you, Brian.' She seemed to be forever thanking him.

'So, what's the problem?'

Lauren took a deep breath. 'It's . . . it's just that he's been going out with my best friend, Anna. I met Glenn when I went to see her in the Bahamas.'

Lauren sighed. 'I'm afraid it's a long story.'

'Go on.'

'If you insist.'

'I do.' Brian patted her hand.

'Well, when I was staying in Nassau, Anna's father was taken ill, and she had to go back to England. I wanted to return home, too, but she insisted I stay and continue my holiday. Her friend, Catherine, showed me around, but then there was a hurricane and I was alone in Anna's flat, so Glenn came round and took charge, making sure I was all right.'

'It must have been scary for you, in a strange country on your own.'

'That's what Glenn thought, so he stayed with me until the hurricane had passed, but by then I . . . I'd fallen in love with him.'

'And Glenn? What did he feel?'

'He said he felt the same way, but I didn't want to betray Anna, she was my friend, so,' Lauren paused for breath, 'so to cut a long story short, I returned to England and tried to forget him, but it didn't work out and it has been disastrous ever since.

'You see, it seems that Anna never loved Glenn. Her former fiancé has turned up and she wants to get back with him, but now she believes Glenn is in love with her.'

'Oh dear, what a muddle. So Glenn turning up tonight, seeing you with me, was probably the last thing you wanted to happen.'

'It was just such a shock. It was so unexpected.'

'Well, let's hope that when Glenn contacts you tomorrow, you'll be able to sort everything out. I'm sure he wants to, otherwise he wouldn't have bothered getting in touch with you again.'

'You think so?'

'I know so.'

Lauren blushed and murmured, 'Thank you, Brian. You're so kind to me.' She was so grateful to him, but at the same time, she felt uncomfortable.

He'd wanted to go out with her on a date, but all she'd done was go on about another man.

'I'm sorry Brian that . . . that . . . '

'You don't need to say any more,' he interrupted. 'I think I knew all along that there would never be anything between us, other than a friendly business relationship.'

Lauren took hold of his hand. 'You're a very sweet man, and if I hadn't fallen for Glenn, who knows what might have happened?'

'Thank you for that, Lauren.'

When they arrived back at the flat, Lauren thanked Brian for a lovely evening.

'The pleasure was mine,' he replied. 'I'll be thinking of you tomorrow and wondering how you get on with Glenn. I hope it all goes well. It's time you had some happiness, I think.'

Impulsively she reached up and kissed him on the cheek. 'Goodnight Brian. And thanks for everything.'

He smiled, watched her walk inside,

waved and then walked away.

She hoped that he too would soon find happiness.

* * *

That night, Lauren had difficulty sleeping. She was worried about the next day. Would it be one when finally all her dreams were realised? Or would she find out for certain that there was no hope for her with Glenn?

She thought back over her life. There had been some happy times, but she'd had her share of sad times, too. The death of her father in a motor cycle accident when she was still a child had been one of them.

But meeting Jake before she was twenty had seemed wonderful. Lauren had fallen for him and thought he felt the same, until the terrible day she discovered that he already had a fiancée.

He told her it was Lauren he wanted now. She didn't know what to believe.

She couldn't decide whether to give Jake another chance, or finish with him.

Then, one day when she was in the supermarket, she saw Jake with a young blonde woman. They were giggling together as they decided which wine to buy. He had his arm round her and they certainly didn't seem as though they were on the verge of breaking up.

Lauren broke up with Jake immediately. He'd protested that he really was going to end his engagement, but she knew better.

It had taken her a long time to come to terms with what had happened. There had been nobody else she was serious about until she had fallen for Glenn, but now she didn't know if she would be able to save the situation with him, or whether she should even try.

She wished that she could discuss all this with someone, especially her mother, but she'd died tragically more than two years ago. There was no-one to turn to. Lauren felt completely on her own.

* * *

She finally managed to fall asleep just before dawn. She woke up at nine as her mobile phone was ringing. She retrieved it from her handbag, where she'd left it the previous night. By the time she'd done this, the caller had rung off. Her heart was thumping wildly. Was it Glenn? Then she remembered he didn't have her mobile number. She saw that it was Anna. Lauren didn't want to speak to her yet. She guessed that her friend was going to tell her all the details about her conversation with Glenn, and what his reaction had been when she told him she wanted to finish with him and was going to see Rob again. Lauren didn't want to hear this. She couldn't bear finding out how upset Glenn was. It was bad enough she had to face him that afternoon.

She had a shower, made a bowl of cereal and tried to concentrate on tidying the flat, but she kept thinking about the approaching afternoon, and seeing Glenn.

Anna rang back during the morning and Lauren felt compelled to answer this time. 'How's everything?' she said. 'I'm sorry I missed your call. I overslept. I was going to ring you later.' This wasn't a lie. She probably would have rung, after Glenn had left.

'I'm fine, thanks,' Anna answered. 'I just thought I'd let you know that I've finished with Glenn. I did it yesterday afternoon. I thought I'd better do it sooner, rather than later. I told him about Rob.'

'You did?' Lauren said, easing herself into a chair. 'And . . . how . . . how did he take it?'

Yesterday afternoon, she was thinking. That must have been before he came round to the flat and saw her with Brian. So what had he intended discussing with her? Could it be . . . ?

'He was OK,' Anna said. 'Very generous, in fact, but I felt terrible about it.'

'What . . . what did he say?'

Anna's answer was important. She might get some clue from it as to what his feelings were.

'He sounded upset at first, but he told me not to worry about him. Then he agreed that it was better to finish now, before things got too serious between us, if that was what I wanted.

'I felt so mean, I had to ask what *he* wanted.'

'And his reply?' Her whole future depended on this, Lauren thought, gripping the arm of the chair.

'He didn't answer. He just said that he hoped it would all work out for me this time.

'It was so hard, Lauren. It was difficult to tell what he was really thinking. He's always such a gentleman. I hated hurting him.'

'So you're back with Rob now?'

'Yes, and I should be really happy, but I keep worrying about Glenn, although . . . ' Anna broke off.

'Although?' Lauren repeated.

'Well, he didn't seem devastated or anything like that, so I wondered if he might have . . . have . . . '

'Have what?'

'Met someone else.'

'Why?' Lauren squeaked. This was something she'd not even considered. While Glenn had been on his travels, could he have met someone else?

'Oh, I don't know. I just had this feeling. I'm probably wrong. Anyway, he assured me he'd be all right,' Anna continued. 'The trouble is, he's so polite, you don't know what he's really thinking. Actually, I'd be relieved if there was someone else. I wouldn't feel so guilty for ditching him.

'I'm sorry, Lauren, to keep involving you in all my problems, but I thought I should tell you what the situation is.'

'Well, thanks for letting me know. So what are your plans now?'

'I've got to go back to Nassau next week. I'll give my notice in as soon as term starts, and I'll work there till Christmas.

'Rob hopes to come out to see me during that time. Then I'll come back to England for good and we'll see how things go. It'll be nice for my parents, too, having me back home. Dad's doing really well now.'

'I'm glad.'

'I'm going to ring up the Education Office tomorrow to see if there's any chance of getting a job here after Christmas.'

'I'm sure you'll find something.'

'Well, if I don't, I can always do supply teaching for a time, until a permanent job comes up.'

'I hope it works out for you.'

'If it does, we'll probably marry sometime next summer.

'And Lauren,' Anna added, 'I want you to be my bridesmaid, unless of course you're married before me, and then you'll have to be my matron of honour.'

'That's not very likely,' Lauren replied, 'but I would like to be your bridesmaid.'

'You never know, you might meet someone and fall instantly in love.'

I did that, Lauren thought, but it hasn't brought me any happiness.

Glenn arrived at two o'clock. As Lauren opened the door to him, her heart missed a beat. In his open-necked shirt and casual jeans, he looked just as stunning as she remembered, despite the grim expression on his face.

'Come in.' Lauren forced herself to smile.

He followed her into the lounge. 'Sit down,' she said formally. 'Would you like a tea or coffee?'

'Nothing at the moment, Lauren. I think we need to do some talking first. Sit down,' he ordered, indicating the chair opposite to him. 'Please,' he added.

Lauren sat down. 'So what have you got to say?' Her words were clipped.

'I think what you have to say is more to the point.'

'Me?'

'Yes, you. Don't play the innocent with me.'

Lauren stared at Glenn in disbelief, her face crimson. She gripped the arm of the chair so tightly her knuckles were white. 'Don't speak to me like that,' she said indignantly.

'I'll speak to you any way I want,' he said. 'After what you've done, I think I have every right.'

Lauren was speechless. What was he talking about? 'I . . . I think you'd better go,' she stammered.

'Go! I came here to talk to you, to try and sort things out. Go? I'm not going anywhere!'

Lauren had never seen him so angry. What had got into him?

'Well, say what you have to and then go.'

'I hurried here last night thinking that at last we could . . . '

'Could what?'

'It doesn't matter now. It's too late.'

'Too late?' Lauren echoed.

'Yes. What did I discover last night?

You . . . going out with someone else, someone old enough to be your father.' Glenn's voice was cold, his eyes steely. 'You didn't take long to find yourself another man, and a rich one too, by the look of him.'

Lauren was furious. The cheek of it! 'I can go out with whom I please,' she stated coldly.

'You led me on, let me believe that you had feelings for me, and then the minute my back was turned, you find yourself someone new. How could you do that, Lauren?'

'I . . . I thought . . . '

'You thought I wasn't good enough for you,' Glenn interrupted. 'You set your sights on someone wealthier. Your boss! I would never have believed it of you. How I was deceived!'

'I never deceived you Glenn,' Lauren said, tears now streaming down her face at the injustice of it all.

'Don't lie,' he said scornfully. 'And turning on the tears won't help, either.'

'I'm not lying. Why won't you believe me?'

'So what were you doing going out with your boss?'

'I knew it was all over between us. I knew you were in love with Anna. I only agreed to go on one date with him, because I was trying to get over you.'

'But I told you I didn't love Anna.'

'I know, but when I saw her with you that day at her house, I knew you'd changed your mind.' Lauren choked back the tears. 'The way you kissed her and made it so plain that you didn't want me there.'

'That was because you'd told me on the phone that you didn't care about me and that there could never be anything between us. I suppose I was using Anna to get back at you. I shouldn't have done it. I'm not proud of myself, but there it is. Anyway, it's not important now, since . . . '

'I only said that,' Lauren sobbed, not letting Glenn finish, 'because I thought

Anna was in love with you and I didn't want to hurt her.'

'We've had this conversation before.'

'I know but I really believed she loved you, until . . . '

'Until?'

'Until she told me she was . . . '

'Going back to her former boyfriend?' Glenn finished for her.

'Yes,' she whispered.

'Precisely. Now you can see why I'm so angry. You let me believe you were in love with me, and then you told me it was just a fling, and you didn't care about me. After that, I tried to make a go of things with Anna, I really did. I didn't want to hurt her, and I thought I might be able to love her, in time. But then she finished with me, and I knew it was you I loved.

'I had a glimmer of hope. I thought that maybe you had said you weren't in love with me out of loyalty to Anna. I thought maybe you did love me, after all.

'So I came rushing here to see you,

and what did I find? You going out with your boss.'

'I'm sorry,' Lauren said. 'I didn't mean to upset you. I've been trying so hard not to hurt anyone.'

'Well, you haven't succeeded.'

'Glenn, please listen to me.' She took a deep breath. This might be the only chance she had to convince him that she'd been speaking the truth when she'd said she cared for him.

'There's nothing going on with my boss. He just invited me out the once and I went because I was lonely. I was . . . missing you.'

'Yeah, sure.' Disbelief was written all over Glenn's face.

Lauren spoke quietly, gripping the arm of her chair. 'Glenn, it's you I love. I've never stopped loving you since we first met.' There. She'd said it.

There was silence. Glenn stared at her. 'What . . . what did you say?'

'I said I love you.'

'You do?' he murmured.

'Yes.'

He got up, grabbed hold of Lauren, pulled her up and put his arms around her. For a moment they both stared at each other and then he kissed her.

He pulled her beside him on to the sofa. 'We've some talking to do.'

'That's what I thought you came round for,' Lauren smiled.

'I did. I'm sorry Lauren, I was so jealous when I saw you with your boss, I lost all reason.'

'There was nothing to be jealous of.'

'I know that now.' He took her hand, kissing each finger in turn, his eyes dark with emotion. 'I think I've loved you since I first saw you at the airport. I've never believed in love at first sight, and certainly never expected it to happen to me.'

'I feel the same.'

'You do?'

'Yes, Glenn. Ever since I trod on your foot.'

'Oh Lauren, now Anna's happy with Rob, there's no obstacle in our way.'

'No. It's like a dream.'

'You're not dreaming Lauren, and I'll prove it.'

Glenn put both arms around her, kissing her until they were breathless.

'You've proved it,' Lauren laughed.

'Now I want to know all about you,' Glenn said. 'What amazes me is that no-one has snapped you up already. You're so beautiful, you must have had dozens of men after you.'

Lauren couldn't help blushing. 'Flattery will get you everywhere,' she smiled, 'but there haven't been dozens of men. Only one who I was serious about, apart from you.'

'Can you tell me about him?'

'I was very young, not yet twenty, when I met Jake. We went out for some months and I thought he loved me, but I was devastated when I discovered he was already engaged. It put me off men for years, until I met you, and then I thought that was going to end in disaster, too.

'But what about you? You must have had other girlfriends. When I saw you at the airport, I thought someone so good-looking must be married, or have a partner at least.'

'Now it's my turn to blush,' Glenn smiled. 'Yes, of course I've had girlfriends, but like you, only one was serious.'

'What happened?'

'Liza didn't like my job. I was always travelling around, and she couldn't cope with that. She wanted someone who worked regular hours, who would be there whenever she wanted. I couldn't give her that, so she finished with me. Then I just had casual friendships until I met Anna. She was different, so English. I suppose that was what attracted me. She also didn't seem to mind my irregular hours or my job. She never made any demands on me and I was happy to let things go on, to see how they panned out. But then you appeared on the scene, and I fell head over heels in love. I felt so guilty and knew that I wasn't being fair to Anna, and everything went disastrously wrong, as you know.'

'Yes, how can I ever forget?'

'I'll make you forget.' Glenn squeezed her hand.

Lauren kissed him, then stood up, 'What about that drink I promised when you first arrived. Would you like it now?'

'Yes, please. I'll have a coffee and tonight I'll take you out for dinner . . . that is . . . if you would like me to.'

'I'd love it. Stay there,' Lauren commanded, when she saw Glenn was about to get up. 'I won't be long.'

* * *

Lauren closed the kitchen door, sat down and caught her breath for a couple of minutes, before making the coffee. Was all this really happening? She wasn't dreaming, was she? Glenn said he loved her, but would it end in happiness? Would he want to marry her, or just have a casual fling? A casual fling would not be enough for her. She couldn't bear it, if it all went wrong now. She forced herself to get up, made the drinks, put some biscuits on a plate and went back into the lounge, where Glenn was sitting where she had left him.

* * *

They spent the rest of the day together, getting to know each other, talking about their childhood and their different backgrounds. Glenn's life seemed so glamorous in comparison to Lauren's rather mundane one in England, but he seemed fascinated by it and listened eagerly to everything she had to tell him. Then, during the evening, he reluctantly said, 'I'm afraid I'll have to go. I've got an early start.'

'Are you going back to New York?' Lauren asked.

'Yes, that's right.'

'I loved Manhattan.'

'I didn't know you had been there.'

'Yes, just a few weeks ago.'

'You were? Who with?'

She replied hesitantly, 'My . . . my boss.' It had all been going so well. Lauren didn't want anything to ruin it now. 'It was business.'

'Oh I see, business.' His eyes narrowed. 'Just you and your boss?'

'Yes. Don't look like that, Glenn. Brian was the perfect gentleman. It was strictly business, although we did manage a bit of sight-seeing. One day I'd love to go back and see it all properly.'

'Would you?' he murmured.

Lauren was hoping that he would suggest taking her there, some time in the future, but all he said was, 'I really do have to go.'

Somehow the atmosphere had changed. Glenn kissed her briefly, but without his former passion. She wanted to cling to him, but didn't dare. 'I'll be in touch soon,' he promised and then he left.

It had been such a wonderful evening until the last few minutes, when it had all ended inconclusively. If only Brian hadn't been mentioned again, Lauren thought. Her earlier feeling of elation was replaced with one of despondency. She wondered how long Glenn would be gone and when he would get in touch again.

* * *

Three days later, during the evening, Anna rang. 'Hi, Lauren. How are you?'

'I'm fine, thank you, but I didn't expect to hear from you until you'd arrived back in Nassau.'

'Well, I'm rather worried.'

'About Rob?'

'No. Everything's fine between us. It's as if nothing ever happened.'

'And you really trust him?'

'Completely. He feels terrible for what he did and promises he'll do everything he can to make it up to me.'

'So he should.'

'No, it's Glenn I'm worried about.'

'Why? Have you heard from him?'

Lauren's heart was beginning to beat faster.

'No. I don't know where he is, whether he's gone back to America or Nassau. I thought he might have rung to let me know he was okay.'

'But Anna, you told him you'd finished with him, so why would he get in touch?'

'I don't know, but I just feel so guilty. I didn't want to upset him.'

'He's a grown man. He can take care of himself.' All four of us have guilty consciences, Lauren thought. If everything works out for Glenn and myself I'm going to have to tell Anna. And that will not be easy. I hope it won't mean the end of our friendship.

Aren't you being a bit premature? she asked herself. You haven't heard from Glenn yet and after the way he left on Sunday night, you might not. But that would be too terrible to contemplate.

'Lauren, are you still there?'

She became aware of Anna's voice. 'Oh, sorry.'

They chatted for a few more minutes and then Lauren hung up, promising to keep in contact by email when her friend returned to Nassau.

* * *

It was Saturday evening before Lauren heard from Glenn. By this time, she was beginning to think he'd changed his mind about her. 'Lauren, how are you doing? I'm at the airport,' he told her.

'Which airport?'

'Heathrow. Can I come over tomorrow? I can't wait to see you.'

'Yes, of course, I can't wait to see you, either.' Her heart was thumping. She was so pleased that he sounded like his normal self.

'Sorry I haven't been in touch before, but life has been frantic. I've been to New York, Nassau and Washington since I last saw you. My dad sure keeps me busy.'

'You must be worn out.'

'I am, so I'll check into my hotel as

soon as I can and get my head down for a few hours. I'll be over in the morning, about eleven. Is that okay?'

'Fine. Shall I make us lunch?'

'If you like, and we can go out for dinner in the evening.'

'How long will you be here?'

'I'm off again on Monday, but I want to talk to you about that. I'd better go now, Lauren.'

'Sleep well.'

'Thanks. I love you.'

'I love you, too. Bye Glenn. See you tomorrow.'

Lauren hung up, feeling so relieved. He'd said he loved her and Brian hadn't even been mentioned. She wondered what he wanted to talk to her about, and couldn't wait for the next day to come.

* * *

Glenn arrived at eleven o'clock exactly. Lauren had been up for several hours, tidying her flat, preparing lunch and trying to decide what to wear. In the end she'd put on a simple lilac dress with a matching shrug.

'It's so good to see you Lauren,' Glenn said, as she opened the door. 'You look lovely.' He hugged her close. 'I'm sorry I was a bit short with you when I last saw you, but I suppose I was jealous, thinking of you with Brian. Do you forgive me?'

'Yes of course, but there was nothing to be jealous of. You do know that? It's you I love.'

She put her arms around him and they kissed until she pulled away, breathless. 'Come inside,' she urged. 'The neighbours will talk if we stand here much longer.'

'I don't care if they do,' Glenn replied, following her into the lounge. 'I want everyone to know that you're my girl. You are, aren't you Lauren?'

His face was anxious. He took hold of her hands, turning her round to face him.

'Yes Glenn,' she breathed, feeling so

happy, 'but I do have to live with my neighbours.'

'For the moment,' he murmured almost to himself, 'but not for too much longer, I hope.'

'Sorry Glenn, I didn't catch what you said.'

'Never mind. Sit down, I want to talk to you.'

She sat down on the sofa and he perched on the armchair facing her. What was he going to say?

'My dad . . . he's branching out into Europe. He's got his eye on some hotels here. He's hoping to increase our portfolio.'

'That's nice.' What has this got to do with me? Lauren was thinking.

'He wants me to sort out all the details for him, so that means I'll be spending a lot more time in the UK. I'm going to rent a flat in London, so I won't have to spend so much time in hotel rooms. I'll have a permanent base in England.'

'That's good.' I'll be able to see more

of him, Lauren reflected.

He got up from his chair, walked over to Lauren, pulled her into his arms and kissed her, when the phone rang.

'Do you have to answer?'

'Yes, I'd better. It might be important.' Reluctantly she moved away, picked up the receiver and said, 'Hello.'

'Lauren. It's Anna.'

'Anna. How are you?'

'I'm fine. I just wanted to let you know I'd arrived back in Nassau, and I've given my notice in at school.'

'That's good.'

'I never heard from Glenn, you know,' Anna went on. 'I'm quite worried about him.'

'Don't be,' he butted in, taking the receiver from Lauren. 'I'm okay. Very well, in fact.'

'Glenn . . . you . . . you're . . . '

'Yes I'm with Lauren. I'm sorry Anna, but you had to know sooner or later, so as you've rung, I thought you might as well know now.'

'I . . . I don't know what to say.'

'Just say you're happy for us.'

'You and Lauren . . . you're . . . '

'We're an item, Anna. Are you OK with that?'

Lauren was standing speechless, then she took the phone back from Glenn.

'Anna. Are you OK? You don't mind?' she asked.

'No. Why should I? I've got Rob.'

'And we can still be friends?'

'Of course. But I thought you didn't like Glenn.'

'I had to let you think that, because I liked him too much. I felt so guilty, Anna.'

'Well you don't need to. This has been a real surprise. I can't believe it. But I think it's wonderful. I really do. Look, I've got to go now, but I'll keep in touch. Bye Lauren. And say goodbye to Glenn for me.'

'I will, Anna. And thanks.'

* * *

Lauren put the phone down and turned to face Glenn. He held out his hand to her. 'Now there's no obstacle in our way,' he smiled. 'Come here, Lauren.'

She walked over to him. He put his arms around her and kissed her. After several minutes, he looked into her eyes and said, 'My father has bought another hotel, you know.'

'Really?' Lauren said, wondering why he was talking about business at a time like this.

'Don't you want to know where it is?' he smiled.

'Well, all right, I suppose so.'

'It's on Paradise Island.'

'Nassau,' she whispered.

'That's right. I'll take you there. In fact, I'll take you to all of my father's hotels, so you can meet the staff. They're always telling me it's time I settled down.'

Lauren stared at him. What was he saying? Was he . . . was he? No. She must be imagining it.

'But I won't take you to one of my father's hotels for our honeymoon,' he went on. 'We'll go somewhere where nobody knows me, for that.'

'Honeymoon!' she cried. 'Did you say, honeymoon?'

'Yes, Lauren. I'm asking you to marry me. What do you say?'

She gazed into the deep blue eyes of the man she loved. She wasn't dreaming. This was real.

'So what's your answer? Are you going to put a guy out of his misery?'

She threw her arms around him. 'Yes Glenn, yes please. And I'd like our honeymoon to be in Nassau.'

He caught her up and whirled her round the room, laughing. Then he stopped and took her in his arms again. He kissed her gently and said, 'A honeymoon in Nassau will be perfect.'

She sighed happily and leant against him. 'It will be our own special journey to Paradise.'

THE END